Happy New Year, Baby

LYNN EMERY

ISBN: 098863032X
ISBN-13: 978-0-9886303-2-1

MORE BOOKS BY LYNN EMERY

Chapter 1

"And Merry Christmas to you," the sales lady said in a weary monotone. She pushed a large bag across the counter.

"I hear ya, girl." Shani nodded her head in sympathy.

The woman, with the name Loreen on a black plastic name tag pinned to her jacket, nodded back. "If I hafta listen to that darn 'Jingle Bell Rock' playin' much longer, they gone take me outta here screamin' like a banshee and ship me straight to the nearest psycho ward."

"Folks shoving and pushing, stepping on your feet to get at the last Ninja Ranger Possum. Or whatever the heck this thing is." Shani held up the overpriced action toy that every child had to have this year. "Not to mention I haven't gotten through half my list yet."

"Tell me 'bout it. I'll be glad when it's over, child." Loreen gave her a long-suffering smile before dropping a receipt in Shani's hand and turning to the next in a long line of customers.

Shani walked to the crowded parking lot. She stood trying to remember which row she'd parked on. After wandering around for ten minutes, she stumbled upon her car. Just getting through traffic away from the shopping mall proved to be an ordeal. By the time she got to her condo, merry did not even come close to describing her mood. All she wanted was to slip into her favorite oversized T-shirt, curl up in the recliner in front of the television, and numb out watching a bad movie. Just as the whistle blew signaling the water for her sugar-free, low-fat hot chocolate had reached the boiling point, the door bell chimed.

"Great." Shani stomped to her bedroom. She pulled on a pair of sweat pants. The triple chime sounded again. "Don't push your luck!" she yelled.

"What kinda greeting is that? What a frown!" Terrilyn bounced in with an armload of packages. "You look like a combination of Scrooge and the Grinch that Stole Christmas."

"I had one lousy day. First—"

"As your best friend I must tell you, leave all that negativity behind. Take a deep breath and say, 'It's over and I can move on and up.' Come on now." Terrilyn put down everything she held and stood in front of Shani. "It's over and ..." She waved her hands like a conductor.

"And as your best friend I must tell you that you're really getting on my last nerve." Shani spun around and headed back to her kitchen. "Hot chocolate?"

"Honey, you could deal with the holiday blues if you gave Dr. Falsum's techniques a chance."

"Terrilyn, don't start with me today." Shani held up a palm.

"I know it's tough getting over a relationship that lasted five years. Especially during this time of the year." Terrilyn shrugged.

"A year ago I was on top of the world. Then it rolled over me like an eighteen-wheeler. But I'm over it. And I didn't need Dr. False either." Shani put the black lacquer tray bearing two mugs on the coffee table.

"That's Dr. Falsum. Okay then, you're fine. Right?"

"Right."

"So what are you wearing?" Terrilyn took a sip from her mug. She looked down her nose at Shani with an air of expectation.

"Wearing where?"

"To the Ladies of Distinction Annual New Year's Eve Ball, that's where. Last year you had a good reason to stay home."

Shani sat back remembering that bleak night. Nothing tasted, smelled, or looked good to her at that time. Efforts by her friends and relatives to lift her spirits only seemed to send her deeper into depression. Her self-esteem had taken a nose dive. For years her sense of worth and attractiveness as a woman had depended on one man. And that one man had rejected her. Terrilyn, as usual, was the one person who said and did the right things. Maybe that's why they had been best friends since high school. Terrilyn let her vent without offering opinions. She allowed Shani to spend the first half of the night talking through her anguish. By midnight they were sitting on Terrilyn's living room floor, on their second bottle of champagne and howling with laughter about some of the things she most disliked about Robert.

"I know it's been said, but thank you for carrying me through that awful night. You were there for me."

Shani gave Terrilyn's hand a squeeze.

"Always, girlfriend." Terrilyn squeezed her hand back. "Now don't change the subject. Today is December ninth; you have less than a month to decide what fabulous outfit you're going to wear. So when are we going shopping?"

Shani took a deep breath. "I can't face that Terrilyn. Robert is sure to be there with Claudia. No, I just can't" She stared down.

"Facing those two is one way to finally close the door on what happened. This is what you do: Get one hot dress, something in black or maybe red. Add one tall, good-looking man, and toss in some new attitude. Strut your stuff on in that place, and what have you got? A recipe for a good time, sugar."

"That's not my style, Terrilyn. I'll settle for a quiet celebration at the Blue Circle Social Club banquet and dance. Mrs. Chauvin invited me again this year."

"Girl pu-leeze! Ain't nobody in that club under the age of sixty. Most of the single men can't dance any-more. Shucks, most of 'em need help walking." Terrilyn wrinkled her nose.

Shani shook a finger at her. "You dated Jesse Fairchild for almost a year. He's a member and not that much older than us. Shame on you."

"Okay, okay. That wasn't very nice of me. But we split up because that twenty-year difference was too much. We're not even in our thirties yet ..."

Shani raised an eyebrow. "Only two years away, babe."

Terrilyn grimaced. "Don't say it out loud. But like I was saying, we finally couldn't agree on anything."

"I'm going to show my gratitude to people who've been a great help to the community center, not to find a husband."

"But New Year's Eve is for celebrating a new day.

A new beginning. To party until you drop." Terrilyn jumped up and begin to move in time to music coming from the radio. "Ooo-wee, let's par-tee!"

"Sit your butt down, girl." Shani laughed in spite of herself.

"The best way to ring in the New Year is with a blast. Think about." Terrilyn did a fancy step as the music ended. "Move on and up, like I said."

"Seriously, one thing you said is true. I'm not going to wallow in self-pity. Instead of acting like the whole world revolves around me and my troubles, I'm going to focus on others. Dozens of people walk through the doors of Mid-City Community Development every day who are a lot worse off than I am." Shani got up to put away the now empty mugs.

Shani's thoughts turned to My'iesha Campbell. That young woman had seen more in her twenty years than most see in a lifetime. Yet she and Shani had connected more than the other drug program participants. The feet that she had dropped out of sight filled Shani with dread. Terrilyn's voice cut through her morbid musing.

"Not work. Oh come on, Shani. You've been spending all your time down at the center as it is. Take time off at least for the holidays."

"Being executive director is not a nine-to-five thing, Terrilyn. We grew up in that part of town. You know how bad it was twenty years ago. Now that crack and cocaine have hit the streets, it's a war zone. There are just so many needs." Shani frowned.

Terrilyn gave a shake of her shoulders. "Yeah, you can't turn on the news without seeing bodies being carried away on stretchers. Horrible."

"Speaking of which, Mr. Carrington said there was going to be a story that might involve Mid-City. You know our board president, he keeps up with

5

everything. It's time for the five o'clock news now."
She turned off the radio with the remote and turned
on the television.

"Got some of those cup cakes with the cherry-
flavored frosting in the middle?" Terrilyn wandered
into the kitchen and opened a cabinet.

"No. You got me hooked on those things and I
gained five pounds in one week. Took me three
months to lose it. You've got the metabolism of a
hummingbird. How you stay a size eight is a mystery
to me." Shani called out

"Got it from my mama. That woman had six kids,
ate whatever she wanted, and only just started
wearing a size twelve. Daddy still can't keep his
hands off her. Honey, it's shocking how those old
folks behave—"

"Shh, this must be it" Shani turned up the volume.

"The Joint Health and Welfare Committee of the
legislature has begun hearings on the looming budget
shortfall estimated by the Legislative Fiscal Office as
over 359 million dollars. It is expected that there will
be significant changes in the next session. The
elections last month resulted in a record number of
conservatives sweeping into office, defeating some
career politicians. One of the most vocal is Eric
Aucoin, the first black conservative to hold office in
the Louisiana Senate since reconstruction."

"Look at that." Terrilyn chewed on a cookie.

"Can you believe it?" Shani glared at the picture
that flashed. A row of legislators stood looking
earnest for the cameras.

"Yeah, girl. He's got it goin' on. My man is wearing
the hell out of that custom-made suit. Umph, umph,
umph." Terrilyn snapped her fingers.

"What? Who are you talking about?"

"That fine brother they just showed."

Shani wrinkled her nose. "I didn't see anything fine in that picture. Just a bunch of insensitive jerks."

"How could you miss Eric Aucoin? Every single woman in Baton Rouge has the hots for the brother." Terrilyn giggled.

"Take a cold shower. That brother, and I use the term loosely, is selling us out. He thinks programs like the ones we have at Mid-City are a waste of the taxpayers' money." Shani snorted in disgust. She made a point of not looking back at the picture. "I've read about him. He's the token black conservative."

"The committee will meet tomorrow to consider those programs and agency budgets that will be reduced." The news anchor, a thin man with iron gray hair, went on to another news item.

Shani turned the sound back down. "Well I'll be there for sure to give them all a few facts about how much money we save the taxpayers. For every kid we keep out of juvenile court or a kiddies' jail with our Teach One, Reach One program, we save the taxpayers over forty thousand dollars. For every addict that stays off drugs by attending our Cocaine Anonymous group we save—"

"Calm down. You better save that intensity for those committee members. But listen, you know how I feel about the center. If I have to, I'll spend night and day with that mean old Senator Aucoin trying to convince him not to cut those programs." Terrilyn wore a leer.

"How kind of you." Shani folded her arms and stared at her.

"Hey, any sacrifice for you my friend. Now all we have to do is get his home address and phone number ..."

"Terrilyn, this is serious."

"You don't think I'm serious about a man with his

7

body? Did you see his chest? Whew!" Terrilyn pretended to fan herself.

"Talk about superficial. It's what's in here that counts." Shani patted her chest. "Obviously he's got no heart for the very people who need help the most."

"Well, maybe you're jumping to conclusions. All I'm saying is I'd be willing to let the man explain himself. Over dinner preferably." Terrilyn grinned.

"Oh he'll explain himself when I get through with him. The committee meets at two in the afternoon. I'll have time to get some work done, attend a staff meeting at nine o'clock, and have a quick lunch." Shani wore a wicked half smile. "I've got his budget cuts all right."

***

The wide hall outside the committee rooms in the basement of the state capitol was jam-packed with people. Shani nodded to several social workers she knew. A perfect swirl of red hair stood out above several dozen heads. Shani wove her way through the mob toward that hairstyle. Soon she heard the distinctive laugh that confirmed the identity of the owner. Paulette Gauthier was considered one of the best substance abuse counselors in the state. She was one of two contract group therapists employed by Mid-City for their drug treatment program.

"Hello, Paulette." Shani gave her a peck on the cheek.

"Hey now. Here comes the cavalry." Paulette put an arm around Shani's shoulders and pulled her close. "Shani, this is Susan Taylor and Joanne Lanier. They work with me at Save Our Streets."

"Hello. Well, what do you think?" Shani nodded toward a knot of men dressed in suits. "The Select

Committee on Responsibility sent their big guns. They must be jumping for joy now that most of the candidates they endorsed have been elected."

"A bunch of men and women born with all the advantages who think they're morally superior to poor people." Paulette stopped smiling. "Look at Ed Parmalee grinning like a Cheshire cat. He's the ring leader, though he keeps a low profile."

"Who are they exactly?" Susan gazed at the distinguished man with a receding hairline and expensive suit.

"According to them they're just a group of concerned private citizens who want good government. They organized three years ago," Shani said. "Ed Parmalee helped them raise over 600,000 dollars from corporate sponsors to pay a consulting firm to study state government. The report just came out two months ago."

"Talk about sending shock waves," Paulette broke in. "They made dozens of recommendations that include major cuts in staff and funding, especially at the Department of Health and Hospitals. Surprise, surprise."

"Staunch conservatives who think government has gotten way too big. They've been pushing for some of these changes for years. Ed Parmalee has been made it his personal crusade," Shani added.

"And now they've put their money to work with ads on television outlining why their recommendation should be implemented." Joanne took up the explanation.

"Yeah, and put up money to back their candidates."

Paulette shook her head. "With the latest round of scandals involving legislators and top state agency officials, the voters listened."

"We're voters, too. So are the people who live in Easy Town and the Bottoms. They're hard working men and women who are due representation just like the folks who live in Sutton Place Estates." Shani spoke with fervor.

"Power to the people!" Paulette grinned at her. "Didn't I say the cavalry was here? Shani Moore, you go girl. We're going to make sure you get a chance to speak."

"You both should speak." Susan glanced around and got affirmative nods from the crowd around them.

Shani swallowed hard. She did not want the ponderous responsibility of being a spokesperson. "I, uh, just came to say a few words about programs at Mid-City they want to cut..."

"Don't be modest. What you have to say applies to us, all of us." Paulette swept a hand around indicating the others. "Save Our Streets has been working to take back poor neighborhoods in south Baton Rouge from the crack dealers and gangs. Grants we've gotten to give kids an alternative are on the line. This is life and death, literally."

"I know." Shani glanced toward the committee room where decisions that could change lives would take place.

"Look, they're opening the doors." Joanne gestured to the Senate aides who had pulled open the double doors.

"I'll meet you in there." Shani did not follow the press of those trying to get in. "Be right back."

The thought of facing such a multitude hit her now that it was only minutes away. She had a strong urge to check her hair and the fit of her clothes. Going in the opposite direction of everyone was like swimming against a strong tide. When someone bumped into her, she dropped her portfolio. White sheets with her notes showered to the floor spilling around the hall.

"Excuse me," Shani said dodging another woman at the last minute. "Great, just great," she muttered as she bent to retrieve the papers from under several large feet. Without warning she ran headlong into a large object.

Seeing the charcoal gray fabric of a suit, she stepped back. Her nose was only an inch from a broad chest. "Excuse me."

"Here, let me help," a rich baritone voice said. "These must be yours, too."

He turned his back to her. In two long strides, he went several feet away to retrieve three sheets she had missed. Shani blinked at the muscular arms that reached down to pick them up. His shoulders rippled beneath the fine fabric. Brown hair in soft waves covered the back of his head and curled over the collar of the dove gray shirt. She drew a sharp breath when he faced her wearing a dazzling smile. Handsome did not begin to describe the chiseled features of his face. The word exquisite floated into her mind even as she examined the full lips and hazel eyes framed by dark eyebrows. But there was something familiar about him. No, I'd remember having met him before. Shani realized with a start that he stood holding out the papers to her, waiting patiently.

"Thank you." She forced her gaze away from him in an effort to collect herself. "Everything goes wrong when you're in a hurry."

"Happens to me, too. I was late getting out of a meeting to get here; took me ten minutes to find my car keys. And they were sitting on my desk the whole time I searched the floor and every inch of the rest of my office." He laughed. "Are you—"

"Senator Raymond is ready, sir." A young man spoke to him in a respectful tone.

"Thank you, Carl." He lingered looking at the floor then at her. "Got everything? I..." A voice began talking into a microphone. "Excuse me."

He seemed apologetic about the need to rush off. Shani felt a sudden gap in the atmosphere when he left, as though the wonderful fresh air surrounding him was sucked away with his leaving. She followed him feeling somewhat dazed by their encounter. A strong urge to be near him pulled at her like a magnetic force. This man she had never met before seemed not only familiar, but someone she knew intimately. With a strange certainty, Shani had a sense that they would like the same music, movies and be able to talk for hours with no awkward silences. Get it together, girl. Seeing Paulette waving her over to an empty seat, she sat down.

"Ready?" Paulette spoke into her ear.

Shani could only nod. She scanned the audience looking for the man who had shaken her tenuous composure. Craning her neck, she looked for the gray suit among the assembly of representatives from community action agencies. There were many familiar faces, but the newcomer was not among them.

"Did you see the tall man in a gray suit? Which agency does he work for?" Shani tried to make herself heard over the buzz around them.

Paulette leaned closer. "What? I couldn't hear you."

"Good afternoon ladies and gentlemen. This is the Joint Health and Welfare Committee. I'm Senator Harold T. Raymond of Sunset, chairman of this committee. We will be hearing testimony regarding items included in the budget for the Department of Health and Hospitals. Specifically, those funded with block grants and Medicaid funds. We have cards with the names of those who wish to present information. If you wish to do so, please complete a card. Each speaker is limited to three minutes."

The chairman continued for several minutes laying out the rules. Shani did not pay attention to him as she was still looking on either side behind her. Convinced she would have to wait until later to complete her search, she faced forward in time to hear the other legislators sitting around the dais introduce themselves.

"Senator Eric Aucoin, district eighteen."

"Oh my!" Shani groaned. Her mouth dropped open.

Paulette touched her arm and frowned at her with concern. "You all right, babe?"

"No, yes." Shani shut her eyes. "Just my luck," She ground her teeth in frustration and anger at herself.

"Huh?" Paulette's arched eyebrows came together in a puzzled expression.

"Nothing. Forget it."

Shani pushed away the warm thoughts of him. Her own harsh words to Terrilyn came back to her. She, too, would do well to look beyond the attractive packaging and remember the threat this man posed to programs vital to poor communities.

The hearings began with Ruth Frazier, the Secretary of the Department of Health and Hospitals, giving a detailed description of the agency's budget. This was followed by fifteen minutes of sharp questioning by the senators. It became clear which senators were sympathetic to social programs and which were skeptical of their usefulness. Shani became angrier by the minute as Senator Aucoin criticized program after program as having shown rapid growth with no evidence that they were effective in reducing the problems they were designed to address.

"With all due respect, Madame Secretary, these programs have shown an average increase of eighty-five percent in the last four years. Yet we've all read in the newspapers that control and regulation of them have been severely lacking." Eric held up copies of the Baton Rouge Advocate and the New Orleans Times Picayune. "Furthermore, even you have admitted that those most in need are not getting the services." Gone was the radiant smile that had so captivated Shani only a short time ago. He wore a serious, searching expression as he waited for a reply.

Though it was only about twenty minutes, the grilling of Secretary Frazier seemed to go on forever. At last the microphone was free for comments from others. Paulette's name was called.

"Senator Aucoin is one tough nut." Paulette pursed her lips. "I'm going to pass. You go." She nudged Shani.

"Hey, wait a—" Shani began.

"Ms. Paulette Gauthier." Senator Raymond called her name a second time.

Paulette stood up. "Ms. Moore will speak next, sir. You should have her card behind mine." She clapped her hands causing a smattering of applause to increase until everyone in the audience joined in.

"Oh my," Shani mumbled.

Now she would have to give up the protective cover of the crowd. Worst yet, she must face Eric Aucoin, an opponent she had drooled over like an overheated moron. She walked to the table dreading each step. She looked up from her notes to find him staring at her with a slight smile. Humiliation and anger flooded her. Shani sat up straight and fixed him with what she hoped was a cold blank expression.

"Good afternoon, gentlemen. My name is Shani Moore and I'm the executive director of Mid-City Community Development, Incorporated. We're a private nonprofit social service agency that operates a range of programs that address needs of the very young to the very old. For example, we have health screening for at-risk infants and home delivery of meals to the elderly. Certainly we acknowledge that mistakes have been made in the implementation of programs. We providers deplore the lack of controls that result in funds being wasted since it means less for those truly in need. But we will not stand by while those who have a conservative agenda use this as an opportunity to plunder agencies that have kept blighted, abandoned neighborhoods from complete despair."

Shani looked at each of the senators in turn. She stared at Eric whose smile began a slow fade.

"Those who should, better than anyone, remember the barriers they faced now suffer amnesia. Certainly as you wield power and enjoy your success, keep in mind that you have left others who still struggle against tremendous odds." Shani pushed back the chair to stand.

"Ms. Moore," Eric said into the microphone in a voice strained with controlled indignation. "Do you have proof that your programs result in *measurable* positive change in the neighborhoods you serve?" He went on before she could answer. "It seems the only answer given by those who favor such programs is to promise results if more money is given. The only real result dependence on welfare, rather than using it as a springboard of opportunity to be self-supporting."

"Senator, it's simplistic to look at such a complex issue as the poverty rate and lay all the blame on the welfare system. Economic and social changes have led to displacement of large segments of the workforce. Not to mention inequities in education and employment opportunities that have existed for generations." Shani spoke in a measured tone yet her dark brown eyes flashed with anger.

Eric shook his head slowly. "It's time for us to take responsibility for ourselves and not behave as victims. What we need is to spend less time wringing our hands about life being unfair and more time working."

His words brought a smattering of applause from the audience and nods from most of the legislators on the committee.

"That's what our agency does, Senator Aucoin. But to ignore the causes of a problem makes no more sense than for a doctor to ignore the origins of a terrible illness. No treatment can be effective without at least an understanding of the forces that work against a cure." Shani's voice rose with force. Loud clapping and voices of assent burst forth. "Most of you oppose our programs without having visited the communities we serve. I challenge you to look into the faces of those whose lives you will change so drastically." She got up and strode back to her seat beside Paulette.

For the rest of the comments she sat stone faced. There was testimony from others who advocated cutting funding for many programs. Many echoed the words of Senator Aucoin. Shani fumed at the man she saw as the worst kind of traitor. The man had no compassion. She glanced up to find him watching her. A tingle went through her body as she gazed into those arresting eyes. With effort, she looked away.

Not again. She was not going to repeat falling for the wrong man. And he was more than the wrong man, they had nothing in common. He was the antithesis of everything she looked for in a man. Not that she was looking. Of course I'm not looking. Now forget it. Stop thinking of that. Shani clenched her teeth with determination to focus on her work and saving the center.

After the hearing was over, she stood in the hallway being congratulated by her colleagues.

"Perfect aim. You hit him right between the eyes with a nice mixture of facts and emotion. I hope the news cameras got that expression on Senator Aucoin face when you started talking. Oo-wee, he was steaming." Paulette chuckled.

"Yes, you were fantastic in there." Joanne nodded.

"As long as they can demonize the poor, their consciences are eased. They give welfare to the rich claiming it trickles down," Shani said. Murmurs of support and agreement fortified her.

As she continued to talk with her friends, Shani pushed away thoughts of his eyes and lips. She welcomed the return of her wrath. How could she feel anything but repulsion for the man? All of the work done for years by dedicated men and women would be undone with one stroke if he had his way. Senator Aucoin was the enemy. And that was that. Shani's small sigh of relief was cut short when a rich voice brought back that tingle. This time it shot up her spine when he spoke right over her shoulder.

"Ms. Moore, I accept your challenge. How's Thursday?"

Shani turned around to find those eyes and lips only inches away. For a heart beat the nearness of him mesmerized her. The tall, muscular frame filled her vision. She felt a wild urge to take his hand.

Paulette's voice brought her back to the present.

"Senator Aucoin, I'm... we'll be happy to meet with you then. Right, Ms. Moore?" Paulette shook Shani's arm.

"What?" Shani blinked at her.

"Senator Aucoin would like to visit the center next Thursday. You have your planner right here. Our meeting with the city Human Services staff was rescheduled. I think you're free." Paulette raised an eyebrow at her.

Shani fumbled with the leather planner, flipping to the daily calendar after several seconds of searching. "Uh, yes. I don't have anything in the morning."

"Good. Ten o'clock?" Eric stood looking down at her. He wore a "put up or shut up" expression.

Shani nodded. "Yes. That's fine."

"Then I'll see you Thursday. Goodbye." He held out his hand.

"Goodbye." Shani steeled herself not to react, at least visibly, before shaking his hand. It did not help to feel the smooth flesh. She assumed the most grim, cool look she could muster.

Eric strode off followed by several other young African- American men. His shoulders moved above most other men through the crowd.

"Well, I thought we were going to need smelling salts for a minute back there," Paulette whispered into her ear.

"What do you mean?" Shani brushed the front of her suit and looked away as they walked outside ahead of the Joanne and Susan.

"Honey, don't even try it. I've known you for a long time. That good-looking man reached out and touched you with those gorgeous eyes. And in more places than just your heart." Paulette laughed deep in her throat

"He touched me all right. Here." Shani pointed to her stomach.' 'I'm still nauseous from exposure to his arrogant, insensitive views."

Paulette held her back. "Y'all go on; we'll catch up," she said to the other two women then faced Shani with a knowing squint. "There was real heat bouncing between you two. Senator Aucoin was checking you out, baby. And he liked what he saw."

"Oh, please. He was fired up all right. Ready to burn my butt and Mid-City." Shani waved a dismissal of her words. She walked off afraid Paulette would see the excitement her words had caused. So, he was attracted to her, too. Interesting.

"Listen to the voice of experience. The passion of opposing opinions, the clash of two strong wills is a potent aphrodisiac. Just don't get swept away."

Shani stopped walking and looked at her friend with a defiant smile. "Eric Aucoin is a legend in his own mind as far as I'm concerned. Don't worry. I won't be used ever again. Not by him or anyone else."

Paulette had scored a direct hit on a sore spot. The hurt Robert had caused her came back with a vengeance. Shani wanted to make it clear that Eric did not have her so enthralled that she could not think straight. But was she trying to convince Paulette or herself?

"Whoa! Excuse me." Paulette eyed her. "Guess I was wrong." She looked skeptical still.

"Yes, you are. And next Thursday will be a day Senator Aucoin won't forget for a very long time. We're going to hit him hard where it hurts. He'll be dizzy for weeks when I'm through with him." Shani smiled with wicked glee as a plan formed.

Chapter 2

Eric stared out the window of his office at the yellow, red, and brown leaves trembling in the chill wind. One hand rested on the pile of papers on his desk. Since arriving in at eight o'clock that morning, he had struggled to concentrate. Somehow it was difficult to make sense of the facts and figures. The rough draft of a bill he planned to submit to the Senate was far from complete. One bill in particular caused his mind to wander. It would result in deep cuts to a grant program that funded community agencies in poor urban areas of the state. The words brought back a vivid image of a beautiful face with dark brown eyes flashing with outrage. Eric was confused by his reaction to her. Based on their encounter, he should want to steer clear of the woman. Yet he kept thinking about her. At odd moments for the past two days she came to mind. Never had he let what anyone thought bother him. He was used to being lambasted by other African-Americans for his conservative view of such issues as the welfare system and affirmative action. Yet her accusation that he did not care about his own community chafed like a piece of sandpaper on a now raw conscience. It disturbed him that she had such a low opinion of his motives. But why? Having dated some of the most attractive, talented women in the state, Eric was peeved that this one female could set off doubts about his positions. Doubts that had never surfaced before.

"Knock, knock." Dalton Aucoin, tall with iron gray hair, strode into the office. He sat down in a large red leather chair opposite Eric's desk. "How are you, son?"

"Fine, Dad. What are you up to this morning?" Eric shifted the stack of files to the side. He hoped his perceptive father would not pick up on his pensive, ambivalent mood.

Dalton Aucoin owed his success in the construction business to his skill at putting up sturdy and attractive buildings at a reasonable cost. But his reputation for refusing to sacrifice quality was legendary. At fifty-six, he had achieved the success his father had always wanted. Dalton liked to tell how he fought his way to the top in spite of being born into a poor family of fifteen children. And as he told his children, he let no one tell him what he could or could not be.

"I had to light a fire under that Tellwood crew. Subcontractors can be a real problem. Before I got so big, Landmark Construction did it all, you know. Oh well, the price of success." His father leaned forward to pluck a several sheets from the pile. He peered at them for several minutes. "See you've made solid progress. Good start, son."

"Yes, I'm still studying some of the research done by the party consultants."

"Any surprises? We know most of the programs are top heavy with high-paid paper pushers. Those folks are more interested in getting plum jobs for their relatives than helping the poor." Dalton snorted with disgust.

"Not all of them, Dad. A few could get rid of administrative layers that are clearly unnecessary. And some have questionable management of funds." Eric thumbed through a report that summarized data on twelve of the largest agencies.

Dalton stabbed the air with a forefinger. "What we need is a better business atmosphere. Lift all these regulations so businesses can operate more efficiently. Profits will go up, jobs will be created, and we can put people to work. Handouts only keep a man down."

"But we do have to have a safety net for some."

"I don't argue with that. There are elderly and disabled folks who need support. But things have gotten way out of hand with all these give away welfare type deals." Dalton stood and glanced at his gold wrist watch. "1 know you'll do the right thing. I'm off to a meeting with the mayor on that urban renewal project."

Dalton waved goodbye without looking back. He hurried off though he would probably be the first to arrive. He was also famous for being punctual.

"Bye, Dad." Eric sighed with relief that Dalton had a lot on his mind this morning. But he could not relax just yet. His friend Chris exchanged a brief conversation with Dalton in the hall then headed for his office.

"What's up, dude?" Chris sauntered in. He was dressed in the latest, casual designer clothes. He draped one leg over the chair Dalton just vacated. Chris had his own telecommunications company. Tel-Com, Inc.'s offices were on the same floor on the opposite side.

"Nothing much." Eric grunted and tapped the folders. "A little light reading."

"Better you than me." Chris wrinkled his nose. "Give me a set of blueprints any day over that."

"Come on. I've seen you handle the most complex government manuals. You could whip through this stuff in no time." Eric took up his familiar theme of trying to convince Chris to run for office.

"No thanks. I'll leave the job of steering the ship of state in your able hands. You've got ideas on how to turn this state around."

"Depends on who you talk to." Eric muttered.

"Yeah, I saw a news clip from the other day. Some lady." Chris laughed.

"Yes indeed," Eric said.

"She sure knew her stuff. Not the impractical do-gooder you were expecting." Chris watched Eric closely. "What's her name?"

"Shani Moore. Eric gazed out the window again. "She works for that big community service agency in Easy Town."

"Lovely name. Shani means 'marvelous' in Swahili. In Kiswhahili it translates as 'an adventure.'" Chris rubbed his chin with a thoughtful expression.

"Really?"

Eric felt a pleasant flush. He thought of the curve of her full lips when she smiled up at him. The perfume she wore was spicy and sweet at the same time. Or was that the natural scent of her skin. It would be nice to get close enough to ... What's the matter with me? Eric shook his head as though to clear it. With a start, he noticed Chris examining him. He frowned and looked at the papers again.

"Ms. Moore has some misguided ideas about what the black community needs. Liberal policies of the past got us into this mess. African-Americans don't need handouts, they need opportunity." Eric spoke in a gruff voice.

"Got to you, huh?"

"Nonsense," Eric said with too much force.

"She is one fine babe." Chris goaded him. "Silky, smooth skin the color of cinnamon. All the right curves in all the right places. Yep, she's got it goin' on."

"She did not 'get to me' as you put it," Eric snapped. "The woman has a mouth on her that won't quit. She all but called me an Uncle Tom." He

23

slammed down a heavy manual, which caused several sheets of paper to fly off his desk.

"Got under your skin for sure." Chris picked up the papers.

"You damn right she did. Any black person who doesn't spout the traditional liberal pap, who shows some sense of being able to think on his own, has to defend his racial credentials. It's preposterous." Eric's jaw muscles clenched. This was infuriating. The woman had him daydreaming about holding her close in one instant and enraging him in the next.

"And you're going to tell her so next week, right?"

"How do you know about that?"

"Trumaine told me. He says you've got a deadline to get proposed bills in so the party can move early in the session."

Eric ran his fingers through his hair. "Which is why I've been working twelve-hour days for over a week now. Trumaine is getting more notes from the lawyers now."

"Senator Raymond breathing down your neck to take a strong stand, eh?"

"He wants to get the wheels turning fast. He's long been vocal about the waste in the budget." Eric thought of the veteran politician who at long last saw his party rise to power on the national and state level. Senator Raymond and other conservatives were impatient to proceed with their brand of reforms.

"This complication won't help then." Chris lifted his hands.

"Complication? What complication?"

"Falling for the opposition. Those guys don't impress me as the kind who would understand that sort of thing. You know, sleeping with the enemy." Chris studied his fingernails.

Eric's mouth flew open. "What . . . No way." He

arranged his expression to be one of relaxed disdain. "Sure she's attractive. But ..." He let the sentence hang, implying he was more than capable of dealing with the wiles of pretty women.

"So the only reason you made a point to arrange another meeting is to set her straight." Chris raised both eyebrows in a skeptical expression that spoke volumes.

"I'm going to lay some hard facts on Ms. Moore that she'll find hard to refute." Eric dug a folder from underneath the others. "When I'm done, she's going to eat her words. When I'm through, she's going to be agreeing with me." He smiled with confidence.

"Smart move. Then getting next to her will be a snap. Still, I've never seen you respond with such... intensity to any woman before now. Ms. Moore is something special."

"Forget it, man. If I was ready to get serious with anyone, and I'm not, it would be someone who shares my values." Eric waved away his suggestion. "My only focus is to make sure we have a reasonable budget and show social workers like Ms. Moore that the old way of tackling social ills does not work. Next Thursday will be a real education for her."

"If you say so." Chris gave an amused grunt before leaving. "Have a good time."

Eric searched for a smart comeback, but could think of nothing to say.

***

"Aunt Shani, look what I made for you." Colin held up a large red Christmas stocking with her name written in gold glitter on it. "It's for hanging on the mantle." His small upturned face searched hers for approval.

Shani wanted to squeeze him tight, but knew better. Now that he was a grown-up ten-year-old, he resisted such gross displays of affection. She was surprised at the tears that threatened to spill down her face. His gift touched her heart.

"I love it, sweetie."

"I made Mama and Daddy and Kara one, too." Colin held up the other stockings.

"Magnificent. Can old auntie give you a tiny kiss?" She could not resist at least one surrender to sentiment.

Colin grinned with satisfaction at pleasing her. He offered his smooth little face before darting off to play again.

Shani sighed as she watched him. She sat in her older brother's spacious den waiting for her sister-in-law to return with their coffee. The radio played jazzy holiday tunes. Shani mused at how much Colin resembled her youngest brother J.J. at that age. A brief spasm of pain touched her chest at the thought of J.J. sitting in prison on Christmas day.

J.J. was serving a ten-year sentence for selling cocaine. Shani and Brendon long ago adopted an attitude of tough love toward him. He was only two years old when their father died and had no clear memory of him. And he was only fourteen when their mother succumbed to breast cancer. J.J. had always been the wild rule breaker of the family. Sadly, he graduated from mischief as a young boy to breaking the law as a teenager. Now at twenty-one, he all ready had a long criminal record. For years Shani spent lots of time and money getting him out of trouble. Brendon finally convinced her that she was enabling J.J. to continue his self-destructive lifestyle.

Shani gazed at the family photo displayed on the bookcase. Brendon seemed solemn despite the slight smile on his attractive dark brown face. While the grief at losing both their parents so soon had caused J.J. to strike out at the world through law breaking and Shani to fight for those in need, Brendon found solace in his career as a computer analyst. He also worked very hard at making a warm, loving family.

"Hello, sis." Brendon patted her shoulder.

Shani blinked in surprise at his presence. So lost in thought, she had not heard him enter the house. "Hi."

"What are you thinking about so hard? All those gifts you got for your wonderful older brother, I hope." Brendon began to sort through a stack of mail.

"You wish," Shani shot back.

"Here we are." Janine swept in. Tall, she still moved with the grace of a model even though she had been a full-time mother since the birth of Kara four years ago. "Hi, baby." She kissed Brendon after putting the tray down on the end table near Shani.

"Hmm, thanks." Brendon took a cup of steaming coffee. "The perfect wife. Greets her husband with a treat when he gets home from a hard day."

"It's the least I can do since you're taking us out to dinner." Janine flashed her famous dazzling smile at him.

"I am?" Brendon laughed.

"I spent all day wrestling with your little dynamo of a daughter while shopping. Thank goodness she's still napping. She wore herself out. Anyway, I got the art supplies J.J. wants. It will be a wonderful surprise for him when he opens his gift."

Brendon's mouth turned down at the mention of J.J. "All that talent and what does he do with his life? Nothing. Worse than nothing."

"Brendon, please." Janine glanced at Shani with a look of helplessness. "J.J. says he wants to turn his life around."

"Sure he does. Now that he's serving hard time." Brendon shook his head.

Shani could see through Brendon's anger to the real pain at losing his brother to the streets. "You did all you could, Brendon. We both did. We were barely out of our teens and still dealing with Mama's death."

"But J.J. has to take responsibility for his choices, too," Brendon said.

"I agree. Still, we could have used something like the 'Lean On Me' mentor program operated by Mid-City." Shani grimaced. "Which is why I intend to fight any cuts to our agency and others like it."

"Let me know if I can help. I'll write letters, send faxes and e-mail those jokers to let them know we won't take it lying down." Janine nodded.

"Thanks, you're a real pearl. Well, I better get going. I have an early day tomorrow and Saturday I'm going to visit J.J."

"Good, you can take our gifts to him." Brendon pressed his lips together and began to open his mail.

"What! You've got to go see him. J.J. will be so hurt if you don't." Shani stood in front of him with her feet apart, hands on both hips.

"Shani, I don't want another Christmas tainted by having to visit a prison. J.J. was in jail this time last year and I bailed him out."

"You're right but—"

"The year before he showed up at my house with a lot of expensive gifts and some hooker on his arm, in front of my children. Expensive gifts bought with blood money. No, my family will have a normal Christmas this year." Brendon's jaw was set in the way that indicated he would not be convinced to alter his decision.

"But Brendon please..." Shani felt the urge to cry return, this time for a very different reason.

"That's final, Shani."

Driving home, Shani tried to be furious with her older brother and failed. The truth was she could not blame him. Brendon had spent more than one holiday traversing the criminal justice system on J.J.'s behalf. Feeling tired and dispirited, Shani put on her pajamas first thing when she got home. She spent the rest of the evening staring at the television. It was midnight before she knew it. Lying in bed for hours, she went over in her head how to tell J.J. Brendon would not visit him.

***

"So you see, we have no choice. Sources tell me Senator Raymond has the votes to push his plan through the legislature." Harold Carrington IV, president of Mid-City's Board of Directors patted his gray mustache with the linen napkin.

The dignified architect sat across from Shani in his favorite restaurant overlooking the Mississippi river in downtown Baton Rouge. He picked at a large shrimp and crabmeat salad while breaking the bad news that several programs would be scaled back July first, the beginning of the fiscal year.

"I don't think we need to make such definite moves yet, sir. We had a lot of support down at the hearing." Shani had pleaded for the better part of an hour. Her lunch, a bowl of chicken gumbo, sat untouched.

"I'm sorry, but we have to be realistic. Walter and I have feelers out to get some limited corporate funding, but for very different kinds of projects.

Batton Chemical prefers less... controversial things such as planting flower gardens to beautify streets and parks. Projects I favored all along." Carrington shook a finger at her.

"And as I've said all along, the problems of the Easy Town are much bigger than cosmetic touches can help."

"When folks have a pleasant environment, they take pride in themselves. It's been done in other cities with great results."

Shani swallowed a lump of frustration. "But we need to focus on more immediate problems first."

Carrington twisted his wrist to stare at his fancy watch. "I have an appointment with some people from New Orleans. I'm sorry to bring bad news and run. But really, Ms. Moore, this may be a blessing in disguise."

"But can we meet later?" Shani tried to get a commitment for further discussion. The look on his face said it would be fruitless.

"I suppose." He shrugged. "I'll get back to you. So long." He left after giving the waiter his gold card to pay for the lunch.

Shani sat alone, oblivious of the chatter of the full dining room around her. Somehow she must make the board members see that giving up was not the answer. She sat brooding over this new menace when a familiar voice jarred her back to her surroundings.

"Ms. Moore, how are you?" Eric Aucoin's posture, he was some two feet from her, seemed to be one of caution. Close enough to be cordial, yet far enough for a graceful exit if rebuffed.

Shani was too depressed for another confrontation. "Fine and you?" she said in a mechanical voice. Her face mirrored the distress churning inside.

"Fine." Eric cleared his throat. "May I join you? Of course, if you would prefer..." He backed up a few inches when her eyes went wide.

"Oh, no. Have a seat."

His request caught her completely off guard. Fortunately, her mother's etiquette lessons put her on automatic pilot. For several minutes they exchanged small talk about the food at Angelle's. Shani recommended he get the soup and salad special. She noticed how his hands, large with smooth skin, made the silverware look tiny. The delicate scent of Armani cologne floated toward her as he waved to the waitress for more iced tea. Eric looked at her and smiled. In an instant, her gloom lifted. Shani smiled back at him.

"So, here we are sharing lunch and you haven't tried to strangle me for being an insensitive traitor to the community." Eric watched her reaction closely.

Shani fingered the cloth napkin. "Yeah, well it's been a bad month. Look, some of the things I said the other day may have been..."

"Insulting? Over the line? Down, dirty, and personal?" Eric dark eyebrows went up. But his lips twitched with amusement.

"Okay, okay. It's just that the programs you're targeting can mean the difference between life and death for some." Shani leaned forward.

"Can you deny some of the abuses that have occurred? Look at that Project Neighborhood Uplift scandal. Hundreds of thousands of dollars unaccounted for. Huge salaries, so-called consultants paid exorbitant amounts to study the needs of the Banks area. Most of the consultants were Marvin Gravelle's relatives and friends." Eric's jaws tightened with outrage.

"I know. But—"

"And that's not an isolated case, Ms. Moore. There is a serious lack of accountability. This voter backlash can be traced right back to the actions of those of you in the human service profession." Eric drew in a deep breath. "I mean..."

"You're right." Shani put down her soup spoon.

"What?" He blinked at her in amazement.

"I've seen darn good programs made useless by so-called leaders using them to pay back supporters. Those of us trying to get the money to folks who need it have been as mad as the voters. But what could we do?" Shani tapped her fingers on the table. "They've got low friends in high places."

Eric threw back his head. Rich deep laughter came out. "I love it. Ms. Moore, you're priceless."

Shani felt a rush of pleasure at the approval in his clear eyes. How splendid to know she could make him laugh.

"Well, we want fiscal responsibility, too. But I'm sure your party members don't think so. And the work we do isn't valued at all I'm afraid." She tried to get back to the subject that divided them to counteract the rising desire inside.

"Talking to you has been a real eye-opener. It seems we share common ground after all." Eric leaned closer to her. "I'd like us to—"

"Senator, I made it after all." A tall thin young man bustled up to their table. "My goodness but Representative Brella can talk. A simple planning session with the other aides became a long lecture when he wandered in to the office. Oh, hello." He stopped short seeing Shani. His voice was cool.

Eric patted the younger man's arm. "Have a seat. Trumaine Delacrosse, this is Ms. Shani Moore." Eric turned to Shani. "Trumaine is a political science major at Southern University. His father and mine were at Tuskegee together. Trumaine is my able assistant."

"Nice to meet you." Shani nodded at the wary young man.

"Uh, are you okay?" Trumaine gave Eric a long, meaningful look.

Shani chuckled. "Don't worry. I haven't hurt your boss."

"In fact, Ms. Moore and I actually agree in a few areas. Something neither of us anticipated. I certainly didn't." Eric gazed at her. Several seconds of silence hung between them. A trill of beeping broke it.

"That's me." Trumaine glanced at his smart phone.

"You're excused to take that call, Trumaine. Go use it." Eric did not look away from Shani.

"Uh, right." Trumaine cleared his throat and stood. He pointed in the direction he was headed. "On my way."

"Wait for me there. I'll be out in a minute." Eric waved at him.

"Yes, sir. Nice meeting you, Ms. Moore." Trumaine wore a knowing grin as he glanced at Eric then at her.

"I really look forward to visiting your center, Ms. Moore." Eric fingered the long-handled teaspoon in front of him. "But I'd like to have more in- depth background information about the origin of Mid- City Community Development and its staff before I get there. It would make my tour more meaningful."

Shani steadied her breathing. Don't be such a fool. This is all business. Isn't it? "I'd be happy to provide whatever you need." She blushed. Shani prayed the possible double meaning of those words that sprang to her mind was not written all over her.

"Excellent. What about lunch on Tuesday? I know a little restaurant on Nicholson that's very quiet.

Rick's would be perfect." Eric beamed at her.

Shani was impressed in spite of herself. Rick's was quiet because the prices on its menu meant only a relatively small clientele patronized it. Though she had never been there, Shani knew it was a favorite among the politically powerful and wealthiest people in Baton Rouge.

Shani checked her planner. "I'm free."

"Then I'll see you Tuesday. Goodbye." Eric held her hand.

Shani felt a tingle at the contact of warmth that spread up her arm into her chest. "Bye." Her voice sounded weak. She cleared her throat. "Goodbye," she said in what she hoped was a stronger voice.

Eric walked away with that long-legged, graceful stride. Shani shook her head. She wondered what happened to her resolve to keep men at arm's length. Eric had chipped away at her wall of resistance. Who was she kidding? He'd blown it away like dynamite with his smile. Well, she would just have to be cautious. But even as she finished her lunch, Shani felt anticipation at seeing him again.

***

Thursday morning dawned bright with promise. Shani sprang out of bed humming to the tune that played on her alarm clock radio. As she went through her routine getting ready for the office, she remembered the lunch with Eric. How right he had been. After a few moments of feeling each other out, they talked for over two hours barely touching the food in front of them. To think, only last week they met for the first time and clashed in front of the entire city! What a difference a few days made. She sang along with the car radio on the drive to work.

"Hello everybody. Umm, that coffee smells good, Elaine." Shani swept past her secretary's desk brimming with cheer.

"Yeah." Elaine exchanged a puzzled glance with another clerical worker. She waved goodbye to her friend and followed Shani into her office. "Mr. Carrington called. You've got a call from Mrs. Lomax; to complain again no doubt. That woman will never get over not being elected chairperson of the Summer Youth Festival."

"Well, we need to be patient with her. She's given a lot of time to the center. Mrs. Lomax is used to having an active role in the festival. After all it is one of our biggest special events."

"Used to ordering folks around you mean. After three years of misery, the committee got up the guts to vote her out." Elaine put one hand on her hip. "Remember how she changed your order on the decorations two weeks before the festival dance? Boy, you were breathing fire." She giggled.

Shani shook her head with a sigh of regret. "Yes, I could have been more understanding."

"You all right? Maybe we should take your temperature." Elaine placed the back of her hand to Shani's forehead.

"I'm fine." Shani pushed her hand away. "Now let me get busy before the senator gets here."

Elaine shrugged and left. For two hours, Shani made phone calls, completed reports, and consulted with staff about the day's activities. Soon it was ten o'clock.

Elaine came to the door and closed it behind her.

"That Senator Aucoin is here." Elaine rubbed her hands in anticipation. "He's on our home turf now. Let him have it, honey." She winked at Shani before opening the door.

Shani came around the desk wearing a large smile. "Welcome to Mid-City Community Center, Senator." She shook his hand.

"Thank you, Ms. Moore. Impressive building." Eric held her hand as he spoke.

"The nephew of one of our founding board members designed it. At a reasonable cost, of course," Shani added. "He's an outstanding architect."

Eric nodded. "Philip Ricard. He's done wonderful work all over the south."

"Let me get you some coffee." Shani went past a wondering Elaine.

Elaine shut the door with care and fell in step behind her to the coffee machine. "Is that the same Senator Aucoin you creamed on television about two weeks ago?"

"I didn't 'cream' him, Elaine. Senator Aucoin has a different perspective on certain issues. We exchanged opposing views." Shani put cream and one teaspoon of sugar in a mug. The other cup held black coffee.

"Say what? Hey, how did you know how he'd take his coff—" Elaine's eyes stretched wide. "Oohh."

Shani wore a mysterious half-smile. She left a now flabbergasted Elaine. "Excuse me."

"Here you are." Shani handed him a mug.

"Thanks. Trumaine should be along any minute. If you don't mind, that is. He'll take a few notes, talk to staff." Eric took a sip of the hot liquid.

"No problem. I hope the material I gave you Tuesday was a help," Shani said.

"Lunch was great. I mean ... very enlightening," he stammered. An embarrassed look of alarm flickered across his handsome features.

Shani felt emboldened by his admission. "I enjoyed it, too."

"Really? Then maybe dinner Friday. If you're not

busy. I mean ... if you're involved with someone. Are you involved with someone?" Eric groaned. "Real smooth, Aucoin."

"It's okay. Yes to dinner tomorrow night. And no, I'm not involved with anyone."

Shani marveled at how easy she felt accepting a dinner invitation. It had taken her months to begin dating after breaking up with Robert. And it was after agonizing indecision. Only a couple of the men had been persistent in pursuing more dates. But both gave up in defeat at the cool, even suspicious treatment they received. Shani was relieved each time when their phone calls stopped. The last date had been over three months ago. Since then she had been careful to give a wide berth to any single man who gave the slightest hint he might ask her out.

"Great" Eric looked up at the ceiling with an exasperated laugh. "I don't usually mumble 'great' to everything like a college freshman. But you've taken me by surprise to be honest, Shani." He gazed at her with an earnest expression.

The dulcet tone of that voice saying her name made her heart rate go up several notches. Shani had to steady her breathing before she could speak. "I have?"

He put down the coffee mug. "Yes. Let's spend time together. I want to know you, really know you."

"I ... I'd like that." Shani soon found her face only inches from his. Elaine's voice made them both start

"I did knock a couple of times." Elaine stuck her head in the door. She eyed them in open speculation.

"Fine, Elaine. What is it?" Shani tugged at her jacket. When she noticed how Elaine stared at her, she stopped.

"The senator's staff person is here."

"Thank you. We'll start with the library." Shani

sprang from her chair and led the way.

For the next hour, they went throughout the building. Shani was gratified Eric seemed to grasp their attempts to support while encouraging self-sufficiency. His questions were thoughtful. Trumaine asked pointed questions about program evaluation, which Shani answered promptly. Eric did not fail to offer support even when Trumaine appeared dubious about the effectiveness of their efforts.

"The center has been open for seven years, right? Hardly enough time to effect lasting change in an area that has been hard hit by a slow economy and drugs for over twenty years. Still you've done a tremendous job." Eric looked around the adult education classroom in admiration.

"Thank you, Senator. By the way, Mr. Delacrosse," she turned to Trumaine. "We have a seventy percent completion rate in our high school equivalency program. Unfortunately, job placement is a much bigger challenge."

"In this job market it's no wonder," Eric put in before Trumaine could speak.

Trumaine snapped his notebook shut as they headed back to Shani's office. "Humph, well that about does it" He arched an eyebrow at his boss.

"Thank you so much for taking time to show us around, Sh..., Ms. Moore." Eric shook her hand.

"You're quite welcome." She walked with him to the lobby.

Trumaine lingered behind. "Looks like I'll be seeing more of this place," he said in an undertone to Elaine.

"Count on it," Elaine whispered back.

"What did you say, Trumaine?" Eric called over his shoulder.

Trumaine scurried to join him. "Just saying

goodbye to Ms. Moore's secretary."

Shani spent the rest of the day dealing with all manner of concerns that usually left her feeling spent and irritated. But nothing could pierce her buoyant mood. After work, she headed for the China Garden restaurant to meet Terrilyn.

"Whew, I'm so hungry. How are you doing, sweetie?" Shani beamed at her friend across the table.

Terrilyn sat back to examine her. "Who are you, and what have you done with the real Shani Moore?"

"Don't be silly." Shani snickered. She waved the waitress over. After ordering, she sat back with a satisfied sigh. "What a great day."

Terrilyn wagged a forefinger at her. "Tell me what you're up to right now."

"I don't know what you mean."

"I've got it! Today you met with Eric Aucoin and publicly humiliated him again. His crushed ego is still splattered all over the walls at the center. Go, girl." She raised her glass of iced tea in a mock toast.

"Actually, it wasn't like that at all." Shani squeezed a slice of lemon in her tea.

"Not one insult?" Terrilyn looked skeptical.

"Nope."

"Not even a little jab?"

"Uh-uh." Shani grinned at her.

"I'm in an alternate universe." Terrilyn closed her eyes for a few seconds before gazing across at Shani.

"Eric seems to truly understand what we're trying to do now that we've met twice to discuss it." Shani watched with glee the reaction to her words.

"Eric?" Terrilyn's mouth hung open.

"He just feels strongly that programs should be accountable to the taxpayers. I can live with that." Shani spoke with confidence.

"I knew it! I just knew you wouldn't be able to resist that tasty morsel of masculinity. Bet I know what area you and Eric agreed on first. Dinner, Saturday night," Terrilyn said.

"Friday." Shani gave a delighted laugh. "It's strange, Terrilyn. After spending time with him, I found out he isn't at all the kind of person I thought he was. He's so . . . nice."

"And you're sure getting next to him is a good idea?"

"Have you heard something about him? Don't tell me he's left a string of destroyed women all over this town." Shani stared at her friend in dismay.

"No, no. He doesn't have that kind of reputation. It's just . . . Are you sure the differences won't become a problem? I don't want to see you go through another letdown." Terrilyn gripped her hand.

"I'm taking it slow, girl. Don't worry." Shani pressed Terrilyn's hand for a second in reassurance.

Still, nagging doubts tugged around the edges of her consciousness as she kept up light chatter through the rest of dinner. Alone at her apartment, Shani pondered all the possible consequences of letting Eric into her life. She made a promise to hold back and not let her heart rule her mind. But the thought of how those large hands would feel against her skin, pulling her close lingered.

***

"This is my favorite restaurant in the city." Eric swept a hand around the dining room.

"It's beautiful," Shani agreed.

Though she loved Lebanese food, this was her first time eating at the upscale Serop's. The carpet was fashioned in rich jewel colors just like a fine

Persian carpet. The chairs were plush and upholstered in the same ruby red, emerald, and royal blue. The soft sound of Eastern music floated around them.

"You're going to love the Mousaka. Of course, the kebabs are great too, especially the beef." Eric pointed to the menu, leaning toward her with enthusiasm.

"I love it all," Shani replied. She could feel the heat from his skin. Not wanting him to pull away too soon, she asked a question. "What about the kebbi?"

"Delicious." Eric's gaze shifted from the list of entrees to her face.

Shani looked up into those clear eyes. "Maybe I'll give it a try," she said in a soft voice.

"You won't be sorry." He put down the menu.

"What will you be having today?" A short round waiter held his pad, pencil poised.

The magic moment, a brief time only the two of them seemed to exist, dissolved. They took their time choosing entrees, exchanging experiences at other restaurants. After ordering, conversation flowed between them. Shani marveled at the comfortable fit of being with him. It did not take long for them to share family histories, where they went to school, and other personal information. She loved to see his eyes light up when he laughed. Or the way his heavy, dark brown eyebrows drew together when he was discussing a serious subject Shani found herself contemplating the joy of being a part of this man's life in a serious way.

"Excuse me?" Shani blushed. She missed what he was saying, so vivid was the image of lying in his arms amidst smooth cotton sheets.

"Hey, look at me. I've been rambling on for so long, you're bored stiff." Eric stared down and fiddled with his napkin.

"Oh no, not at all. I'm sorry, I was just thinking . . ." Shani hesitated. She did not know how to go on. How to tell him without coming on too strong? *I can't believe I'm here feeling like this. I hardly know the man.*

"Yes?"

"This is so strange. A few days ago I wanted to slash your tires and publicly humiliate you. And now I'm laughing at your jokes." Shani gazed at him.

"And I know my jokes aren't that funny," he said with a grin. "So that means we like each other. We're Eric and Shani, not Senator Aucoin and Ms. Moore." He took her hand.

Shani felt sweet yearning flow through her body. A yearning stronger than she had ever felt before, not even for Robert. "You're very different from how I imagined you to be."

"I haven't evicted any widows or taken candy from a baby in weeks." Eric's eyes twinkled with mirth.

"See, I've had a positive influence on you all ready." Shani giggled. "You might even vote liberal next election."

"Hey, let's not get carried away." He let out a musical laugh. "Maybe you'll vote conservatively."

"Depends on the candidate I guess." Shani's eyes softened with affection.

Eric gazed at her. "I want to spend more time with you, Shani. There's something strong between us."

"I feel it, too. But you don't think our views will be a barrier?" Shani wanted to touch his face.

"Not if we talk it out. I don't know any couple who agree on everything. Besides, it's worth it. Well?"

"Let's do it. I mean ... uh." Shani's eyes went wide.

"We'll get to know each other, not . . ."

Eric stroked her hands to calm her fear. "I don't want to rush anything this important."

"Me either." Shani stared at their entwined hands. His touch both comforted and excited her.

"Now what do we do?" Eric smiled at her.

"I've got an idea. Let's go downtown to see the Christmas lights." Shani wanted to share one of her greatest pleasures at this time of year with him. Being with him would make it even more so.

"You've got it. I haven't done that in years." Eric's face brightened at the prospect.

They strolled around the governmental complex admiring the lights and displays set up by the city. Shani loved walking beside him, her arm looped through his. They bought hot chocolate from a street vendor. They even danced the two step as a Zydeco band played on the levee plaza overlooking the Mississippi River. The huge bridge spanning the river between Baton Rouge and Port Allen was strung with white lights that shone against the deep blue night sky. Shani felt a kind of enchantment in the air. When they returned to Shani's apartment, he came inside but would not stay.

"I had a fantastic time. But it's time to go." Eric stood near speaking low.

"You're working on Saturday even?" Shani felt dazed by the force of his presence.

"Yes, but that's not why I'd better leave. Believe me taking it slow with you isn't on my mind right now. Goodnight, Shani." He covered her lips with his, exploring with slow movements.

"Goodnight," Shani said.

From the moment the door closed behind him until she sank beneath her down comforter, Shani relived the sensation of his kiss. Being in his arms was more electrifying than she'd imagined. Yet she relished the process of getting to know him. It would make the first time they made love even more passionate. The days ahead seemed luminous with the promise of love.

Chapter 3

The sky was several shades of gray, dark lead to silver in spots. A fine mist hung in the air. Shani shivered even though the heater in her Toyota Camry was working well. Trips to the Angola State Penitentiary sent chills through her no matter what the weather. She would never get used to this. The long winding drive only added to her dread each time she went to visit her younger brother. It was depressing in the summer when the trees and bushes of rural West Feliciana parish were resplendent in deep green, sunlight painting the rolling hills bright yellow, and blue skies stretching for miles. Then she thought of how much J.J. loved the outdoors. How awful that he had to see such beauty from such a dreary place. But today the scenery was a perfect match to her mood.

Shani went through the routine search at the gate. She was searched again before she was allowed into the visiting area, a large room scattered with tables and hard metal folding chairs. Four or five guards took turns strolling around the big room or standing along the walls observing. All the prisoners were dressed in pale blue denim shirts and dark blue jeans. J.J. wore a crooked smile that was a shadow of the radiant boyish one he'd once had. Shani could see the progressive change with every visit during the first six months of his sentence. His face was thinner and his eyes dull.

"Hello, J.J." Shani hugged him tight.

"How ya doin', baby. Whew! Look at you. Getting prettier every year. Just like Mama." J.J.'s face softened for a few seconds before the veil of hardness came back. "So how's the family?"

Shani shifted in her chair. "Doing fine." Too soon to tell him Brendon would not come. "The kids are growing like weeds."

"Wish I could see Colin. And Janine was pregnant with Kara when I was sent up the first time."

Shani brought out the small photo album. "Voila. The Moore family in all their glory."

"Oh, she's lovely. My main man Colin." J.J. drank in the photos like a man taking a refreshing drink after being parched for a long time. "Brendon and Janine always did make a good-looking couple, didn't they?"

Shani glanced at the picture of the two sitting on her living room couch, Brendon's arm draped around Janine. "Yeah, they do." Shani bit her lip. Now?

A full minute passed before he spoke. J.J. did not lift his head, but continued to gaze at the photo. "He's not coming, is he?"

"No, he's not coming." She put a hand over her mouth to stifle moan of sorrow. Her family, already left with a huge hole caused by the death of their parents, was slipping away it seemed.

J.J. straightened one or two photos then closed the album with care. "I understand."

"Well I don't." Shani fumbled for the purse-sized pack of tissues she knew to always have on hand for these visits. "It's enough that you're locked up for what you did; Brendon is wrong to punish you this way." She wiped tears from her eyes.

"Shani, listen to me . . ."J.J. said taking her hand.

"No, J.J. I won't forgive him for deliberately hurting you."

J.J. held her hand for several minutes until the quiet sobs tapered off. A burly, black guard approached.

"Everything all right here, ma'am? Y'all need anything?" He eyed them with concern.

Shani, expecting some censure, feared for J.J. The compassion in the big man's rugged face touched her. "I'm okay, sir. Really." She sniffed.

"Thanks, Officer Crawford. Come on now. Cut that out." J.J.'s voice was tight with emotion. "You're being too hard on Brendon. Besides, what kind of role model am I for Colin? Brendon is trying to raise two kids in a world that's got high mountains for black boys to climb."

"What kind of message does disowning his brother send to Colin and Kara?" Shani said with force.

"Shani, I don't think you realize how much I hurt him." J.J. sighed. "When Daddy realized he was dying, he had a talk with Brendon. He was only nine years old, still he took that promise as seriously as any grown man. In Brendon's mind he's not only failed me, but Daddy."

Shani's breath caught in her throat. "J.J., I never knew..."

"All these years every mistake I made weighed on him like they were his, too. Brendon can't face me, Shani. And it probably scares the hell out of him that he'll repeat his failure with his own children." J.J. took a deep breath.

Shani gazed at him with new respect. "J.J., I've never heard you talk like this."

"You mean think about somebody other than me for longer than three seconds?" he said with a grin that almost recaptured his youthful fun-loving expression.

"I'm embarrassed you had to tell me, a clinical social worker by training, what should have been obvious all along. You are one perceptive man." Shani took his hands in both hers.

"Shani, tell Brendon how much all he tried to do

for me meant. Maybe I didn't see it then, but now I do. The one thing that has made a difference is remembering all the ways he stood by me." J.J. sat up with his shoulders back. "I'm going to earn back his trust, respect, and love. I'll make you both proud of me."

Shani brushed his chestnut brown face with her fingertips. "You don't need to earn our love, J.J. That's something I can say for both of us."

For the first time since coming to the prison, Shani left with spirits higher than when she arrived. The crowning good news was J.J. felt sure he would be released on parole in January. The parole board would meet in another week to consider his request. Based on his good behavior, recommendations from several ministers and others, the chances were good he would be home before mid-February. She said a silent prayer of thanks. As she crossed the boundary line back into East Baton Rouge Parish, Shani swore again to build up the children's programs at Mid-City Center. She thought of all the boys who had no one trying to lead them in a positive direction. But there were people ready to reach out. Shani thought of the men who spent time with young boys at Mid-City's recreation rooms. And now she could look to Eric for help. The memory of him sent a thrill up her spine. How marvelous to know they would be fighting together against forces tearing the African- American community apart rather than each other. Thoughts of sharing Christmas with Eric planted a smile on her face.

Everyone at the office marveled to see her breeze through several trying situations with uncharacteristic ease. Elaine shot sidelong glances at her when she thought Shani was too busy to notice. The secretary almost dropped the morning mail when she returned to find Shani humming "Jingle Bell Rock" and taping Christmas cards to her office door.

"Look, Elaine. This one is my favorite," Shani said waving a card with a large white dove in flight surrounded by embossed green and gold foil paper shaped to resemble ribbons. "Of course, this one with the little kids listening to a bedtime story is so cute."

"Yeah, it is." Elaine scratched her head. "You feeling okay, Shani?"

"Certainly, Elaine. Now it's perfect." Shani stood back to admire her handiwork. The colorful cards against the background of red, green, and gold wrapping paper did brighten up the place. Shani made one last minor adjustment before going to her desk, still humming.

"Hi, Jesse." Elaine's beginning smile of greeting froze at the look on his face.

As head of operations and maintenance, Jesse supervised janitorial staff. He also made sure the building was kept in good condition.

"What's wrong?" she dropped her voice. The short muscular man gave a grunt of vexation.

"We gonna hafta fire Carlina Brown. I caught that woman loading some of the food from our kitchen into her trunk. Had the nerve to give me attitude when I told her about it."

Elaine screwed up her plump face. "Oh man! You're coming in here to mess up her good mood. For the first time in months she hasn't been snappish."

Jesse threw up his hands. "Hey, don't blame me. She's got to know this. I can't fire nobody without telling her. I ain't lookin' forward to it neither."

"Hi, Jesse," Shani called through the door. "Merry Christmas."

Jesse looked up at the ceiling. "Why did it have to be me first thing this mornin'?" he muttered in a low voice.

"Hi, Shani. Merry Christmas. 'Course you ain't gone be so merry when I tell you what I have to tell you."

"He's a damn lie!" a gruff voice yelled. Carlina, thin and wiry, marched past Elaine into Shani's office.

"What's going on?" Shani glanced at Jesse then at Carlina.

Carlina jabbed a finger at Jesse. "This no good dog is a liar, that's what's goin' on. Them was bags Miz Craig told me I could have," she shouted.

"Lower your voice, Ms. Brown." Shani closed her office door. "Now, Jesse—"

"I been working 'round here off an' on for four years. He been on my case since I got here." Carlina started blubbering. "It ain't right, Miz Moore."

Shani handed her a wad of facial tissue. "Let me—"

"You ain't no good, Jesse. You know you wrong." Carlina said, her voice muffled by the tissue. "Miz Moore, I need my job."

Jesse shot her a smoldering look of condemnation. "Last month I saw her puttin' some liquid cleaner from the storeroom in a big bag. She saw me watching and put it back."

"That's a da—" Carlina broke in.

"Be quiet please." Shani held up one hand. "Go on, Jesse."

"She tried to tell me she was goin' to clean, even though it was five minutes before quittin' time. Claimed she hadn't noticed what time it was. I let her go with a warning to be sure all materials was put away before she left."

"What he doin' spyin' on people anyway? Musta been scared somebody was gonna see him do somethin'." Carlina glared at him. "Betcha you search his house you find some center stuff."

"I don't need to be no thief," Jesse spat at her.

"That's enough," Shani said in a commanding tone. She stood between them. "We can settle this. We'll have Mrs. Craig confirms she gave Ms. Brown permission to take the food."

"Here she is now." Jesse wore a look of satisfaction. "I asked her to come, too."

Lucille Craig, the short, round kitchen supervisor, came in still wearing a hair net and apron. "Mornin', Miz Moore." She nodded to the others. "What y'all need?"

"Did you tell Ms. Brown she could have those bags Jesse saw her loading into her car?" Shani folded her arms.

"Sure. She said she could use 'em. No sense letting it go to waste." Mrs. Craig shrugged and then frowned seeing Jesse's expression. "What's wrong with that?"

"Nothing. We'll talk later." Shani meant to point out that helping employees in need was admirable, but should be done after consulting with her to avoid just such a misunderstanding. "Well that's it then. Jesse, it seems Ms. Brown was not stealing the food."

"Told ya so." Carlina gloated. Her eyes sparkled with malice. "Now I want him wrote up for startin' this mess."

"How was I to know Miz Lucille gave her all that meat and stuff?" Jesse mumbled.

"Meat and stuff? I ain't gave her no meat. And what else you sayin' she had in them bags?" Mrs. Craig's question caused them all to freeze for a few seconds.

Shani looked at Carlina, whose gaze darted around the room as though searching for an escape route. "Jesse, tell us exactly what was in the bags."

"Two canned hams, frozen chicken legs, three

boxes of powdered milk ..."

Mrs. Craig placed both hands on her hips. "All I put in them bags was some vegetables. They from my uncle's farm an' we had more than we needed for the dinners. I brought 'em intendin' to share with some of the workers."

"Uh-huh! Just what I figured." Jesse planted two meaty fists on his hips.

Mrs. Craig faced Carlina with a glower. "You decided to get slick an' pack them bags with other food. Come to think of it, food been dissappearin' for three months now. Ever since you come back."

"Sure has, Miz Craig," Jesse put in.

"Thank you, Mrs. Craig." Shani gestured for her to leave.

"You welcome. Humph." Mrs. Craig threw Carlina one last look of scorn before walking out.

Shani faced Carlina. "Ms. Brown, you are terminated effective today. Elaine will prepare your last paycheck." She opened the door and stared at Carlina.

Carlina shot them both a venomous look before stomping out and down the hall.

"Thank you, Miz Moore." Jesse started to leave. "I hate this happened. By the way, that guy was over here a few days ago been wanderin' around the halls. He's in the library now I think."

Shani's heart skipped a beat. She headed for the library full of anticipation. Her face must have shown obvious disappointment when she found Trumaine chatting with the librarian.

"Sorry, just me," he said. "I decided to take more time to fully investigate, I mean, explore all facets of the community center. To make sure all the work you're doing here gets adequately presented in my report." He flashed a winning smile.

Shani shook his hand. "You're welcome anytime, Mr. Delacrosse."

"Trumaine, please. Miss Zeno was telling me about your story hour for children. What a wonderful oasis in a desert of crime and immorality." Trumaine shook in head.

Shani felt a streak of irritation at the condescension in his tone. "There are hundreds of hard-working, church- going people in Easy Town. Being poor doesn't equal moral deficiency."

"Of course, I didn't mean all residents. But crime is rampant. And most households are headed by unmarried mothers who can't get the fathers of their children to support them." Trumaine held up a sheet of paper. "It's here in the grant proposal your organization prepared."

He held a copy of the center's application for a Ziegler grant established by the wealthy Louisiana family of the same name. Shani wanted to snatch it from his hand and hit him with it. Unlike Eric, the more she got to know Trumaine the less she liked him.

"It's wise to appreciate that a community is more than a compilation of statistics and graphs. You have to walk among people to really understand their plight." Shani kept her voice calm. She even managed a smile.

"Which is precisely why I came back for another visit," he replied in a suave manner. "Well, I think that should about do it. Thank you so much for allowing me to impose, Miss Zeno. Goodbye Ms. Moore."

Shani grimaced at his back as he left. "What was he asking about exactly, Denise?"

"What kind of special events we have here at the center, who my boss is, things like that. He was only in here a few minutes before you came, Shani."

Denise wandered off to help a teenager in the reference section.

Shani walked back to her office slowly. Why was Trumaine snooping around? Something about Trumaine Delacrosse disturbed her. She had a feeling he was looking for dirt. Maybe she had been wrong to assume Eric would break from his conservative leanings. For the rest of the day she went over their previous conversations. She was still feeling wary when he picked her up for dinner.

"Hello." Eric pecked her cheek lightly. He was impeccable in a heavy wool sweater the color of burgundy wine, navy pants, and leather loafers the deep red color as his sweater. "Looks like we're going to have cold weather for Christmas."

"Hi. Have a seat. I'll be ready in a minute." Shani went back to her bedroom.

"In fact the weatherman says we're going to have cold weather through New Year's Day. Perfect for the holidays," Eric called to her.

After several minutes, Shani came back into the living room with her purse and sweater jacket. "Yes."

Eric stood and pulled her close. "It's going to be a very special Christmas for a lot of reasons," he murmured into her ear.

"Will it?" Shani's face was impassive.

"Um-hum. And you're most of them." Eric nuzzled her neck with his lips.

The faint brush of his mouth on her skin set tingles of desire through her. Yet the suspicions brought on by Trumaine's visit to the center caused Shani to tense. "I'm really hungry. Let's go."

Eric blinked in confusion. "Wait The temperature is pretty low in here, too. Have I done something wrong?"

"No, it's... Forget it. You ready?" Shani tried to

move away, but Eric tightened his hold.

"We're not leaving this apartment until I get some answers. Now talk to me," Eric said. The firm set of his jaw gave his handsome face stern look.

"Your fact finding seems to be very meticulous, Trumaine Delacrosse made a second visit to Mid-City without letting me know he was in the building." Shani bristled at being treated like an errant child. "More like he was digging for dirt."

Eric loosened his hold. "Honey, is that all?" He smiled.

Shani grew even more incensed by what sounded like a patronizing note in his voice. Honey indeed! She put several feet between them. "All? Do you think this is some game I'm playing? Funding for programs that are critical to that community are under attack. Don't imagine we haven't been through this enough to know some of the tactics you've used."

Eric grew serious again. "Now wait a minute—"

Shani pressed on as her angered gathered steam. "You take things we tell you, and turn it against us. Maybe I've been a bit naive."

Eric stood with his feet apart and arms folded over his broad chest. "Shani, you are—"

"Trumaine knew exactly what to look for on his second visit, I'll bet. He looks like a real budding spin doctor or should I say junior hatchet man?" Shani faced him full.

Despite her words, Eric appeared calm. His voice was even when he spoke. "Can I say something now?" When she said nothing, he walked to her. "I'm sorry Trumaine didn't go by your office first, but your administrative assistant told him it would be okay."

"Elaine?" Shani was taken aback.

"Yes, Elaine. She was sure you wouldn't mind since you did tell us both we could visit to get information anytime." Eric placed both hands on her shoulders. "Trumaine told me he missed a few details during the first tour."

"Oh." Shani let her arms fall to her side. "I didn't know."

"Let's sit down for a second." Eric pulled her over to the sofa. "It is very important that you believe what I'm about to say. We don't agree on some issues, but that's not news to you. If I ever oppose anything that involves Mid-City Community Development, Inc., you'll be the first to know." He wrapped a muscular arm around her.

"Eric, I'm sorry I jumped to con—"

He put a finger to her lips. "I'm not finished with you, woman." His face was inches from hers. "What I feel for you is so strong it's hard to put into words. And nothing is as important to me right now. I want, no, I need to have you in my life."

A heat wave started in Shani's toes and traveled up taking full control of her body. Strong was an understatement. This feeling eclipsed anything she had felt before for a man. She felt giddy with desire, willing to risk all. Watching his full, delectable mouth hover ever closer mesmerized her. It took considerable effort to speak.

"When I saw you the first time that day at the state capitol, I felt ... so good being near you," Shani said in a small voice. She struggled to put into words the strange magnetism he exercised over her.

"Yes, so very good. And it's been growing ever since," Eric said.

Eric's touch was tender as he caressed her face. He kissed her long and hard. When they parted, both were breathless.

Shani fell back against the large cushions. "My oh my." She fanned herself.

Eric puffed a few times. "Have mercy."

Shani's eyes were aglitter when she looked at him. "There's a great Chinese restaurant nearby. They deliver."

Eric closed his eyes. He pressed his lips to her forehead. "I love Chinese takeout," he murmured.

Dinner was a delightful game of tease. Shani took great pains serving their plates. They sat across from one another at her dining table. She lit candles that gave off a mild scent of spice that went well with the meal.

"Umm, this shrimp Schezuan is tasty." Eric put down his fork. "But I'm stuffed." His plate was more than half- full.

Shani savored a helping of moo goo gai pan. "China Garden is the best in town. Is that all you're going to have?" She pointed to his plate. "Have another taste."

"All right, I will."

He came to her in one quick motion and lifted her up from the chair. Swinging her around in slow motion to the rhythm of a blues ballad playing soft and low, he let his tongue roam across her lips. Pressing her body to his, she matched his movement to the music. Shani no longer wanted to play the game. She wanted to feel his bare chest against hers. Her hand guided his fingers to the front buttons of her sweater.

"What about going slow?" Eric said between short gasps.

"Oh we will definitely go slow, sugar. Nice and slow." Shani led him to the bedroom.

True to her word, even their undressing was a sweet, sensuous ceremony. Shani ran her tongue down the middle of his chest and around each nipple until he cried out. Yet still she took her time as they stood naked in front of the full length mirror near her bed.

"What are you doing?" Eric watched in fascination. Her hands moved over his body without touching the one spot that ached the most.

"I'm taking my time," she whispered, her mouth against the flesh of his shoulder. "I want you so bad, baby. But I don't want this to end too fast." Shani made the act of wearing the condom an act of erotic play.

She pushed him down on the bed. Eric moaned deep in his throat as she lowered herself onto him. The gentle rocking motion propelled them both to cries of pleasure. The lingering motion went on for a long, luscious time until Eric began to buck beneath her. With one elbow braced on the bed, he lifted his pelvis while clutching her waist. His thrusts sent shudders through her. Shani dug her fingernails into his shoulders.

"Now, baby," Eric said through clenched teeth. "Now."

Shani let control of her passion slip just enough. Ecstasy raked her body like thousands of needles. Tiny needles of both pleasure and pain.

"Please, please. Oh, Eric!"

His cries were a mixture of grunts and groans incomprehensible except for her name repeated with each bone shaking stroke as he climaxed. Shani crumpled in a heap on his chest. Eric eased her down to stretch beside him on the sheets. Minutes stretched into an hour before either spoke.

"Now that you've seduced me and made me into an obsessed man ..." Eric began.

"Say what?" Shani poked him in the ribs.

"That's right, young lady. You have to take responsibility for your actions and do right by me. I'll need treatment." Eric combed his fingers through the tangle of her thick hair.

"What kind of treatment?" Shani snuggled into the crook of his arm.

"Regular doses of your voice, your face, and . .." He squeezed her thigh beneath the sheet. "Everything else your hot little imagination can cook up."

"Well under the circumstances it's the least I can do." She giggled.

"Good. And about our politics," he said lifting her face to his, "Don't ever suppose what I believe could lead me to intentionally hurt you. Promise you'll trust me, Shani," he whispered.

"I promise, baby. I promise." Shani gave him an ardent kiss that rekindled smoldering embers.

Chapter 4

"Hey good-lookin'." Eric planted a solid kiss on his mother's cheek.

"Hello, dear," Adeline Aucoin said. She gave him a maternal pinch of his cheek in return. "Well, you look okay I guess. Getting plenty of rest?"

Eric shrugged. "Enough. I try not to work late too many nights in a row. Yum-yum, you've been baking again." He reached for a plate of brownies under a round glass cover on the kitchen counter.

"Your favorite." Adeline beamed at his sighs of satisfaction.

"You must be feeling pretty good then."

Eric gazed at his mother, searching for signs that she was in pain. Adeline suffered from rheumatoid arthritis, high blood pressure, and asthma. Though she had never been strong, her health had grown worse in the last four years. There were days she could not get out of bed without assistance. Dalton Aucoin treated his wife with a tender concern in stark contrast to the brusque manner he usually displayed.

"Tip top." Adeline smiled at him. "Really dear, you shouldn't worry about me," she replied seeing the small crease remain in his forehead. She patted his arm to reassure him.

"What did the doctor say?" Eric knew from his father that she'd had her checkup the previous day.

"I'm doing well all things considered, baby." To prove her point, she walked over to the refrigerator. "You need something to wash that down."

She poured him a glass of milk much as she'd done when he came home from school as a boy. Adeline sat next to him at on a stool. With long fingers showing slight swelling from arthritis, she arranged the ankle-length green silk lounge dress. Her hair was a lustrous silver gray perfectly styled. Adeline was meticulous with her hair, makeup, and dress. And despite her illnesses, she was still a handsome woman at fifty-three.

"Now I want to catch up on you. How is work coming along? I hear a real fight over the budget is shaping up."

"Yes, a lot of sacred cows are on the carving board. It's not going to be pretty or polite this session," he said referring to the upcoming legislative term. "There are some pretty determined folks on both sides."

"Indeed. One in particular seems to have made quite an impression. On the media, I mean." Adeline pretended not to notice his darting glance.

Eric cleared his throat. "Oh? Think I'll have some more milk." He went to the refrigerator.

"There to your right on the top shelf," she pointed to the red and white carton. "An attractive, articulate young woman was shown tearing into you at one of your committee meetings. Now what is her name? Morton, Morrison ..."

Eric came back and gave her an admonishing look. "Mama, let's cut the cat and mouse game. You've got a better pipeline of information than the FBI."

Adeline looked innocent. "Why I don't know what you mean."

"Mama." Eric stared at her hard.

"Well it just so happens my friend Imogene Hampton's son is a member of the Mid-City Board of Directors. She says ..." Her voice trailed off at his frown. "I wasn't being nosy. Immy and I got to talking one day over coffee after garden club meeting."

"Sure." Eric looked skeptical. "And it just happened to come up."

"Immy might have said she saw you two having lunch." Adeline fussed with her hair. "Of course I told her she must have been mistaken. Eric would most certainly have introduced me to her, I said."

"Mama, we only started seeing each other a few weeks ago. And you haven't met every woman I've dated in the last seven years."

Adeline's finely shaped eyebrows went up. "Only the two you were serious about. Or thought you were serious about. Thankfully you came to your senses both times."

"Mama—"

"I know you too well, Eric Paul Aucoin. If it meant nothing, you would have mentioned having met her over lunch when I first brought it up." She waved a finger in front of his nose. "She seems to a *nice* young woman from all I hear." The word "nice" was said in a disparaging tone meant to provoke him into talking. It worked.

"Shani is a caring committed professional and yes, Mama, she is a very *nice* person; someone who cares about other people. Unlike most of the silly women you've shoved at me." Eric wore a sour expression.

"I don't shove women at you, Eric," Adeline said in an injured voice. "I've merely introduced you to some of most beautiful young ladies from the finest families in Baton Rouge."

"With nothing heavier on their minds than the next shopping trip in New Orleans or Houston."

"Don't be ridiculous. Jalisia Minor is a top marketing consultant. Why you don't see her anymore is a mystery to me. The poor girl adores you."

"Jalisia works, if you can call it that, for her uncle. She's looking for a husband so she can explore new frontiers of credit," Eric retorted.

"Nonsense. And what about Helene Cavalier? She's the top assistant to the secretary of the Department of Health and Hospitals."

Eric laughed. "Who made it clear when we first met that she had an income requirement for any man she'd let in her life. Don't get me started, Mama. I could tell you things about those lovely ladies that would curl your hair."

"Don't be crude, Eric." Adeline looked away in an attempt to hide the spark of interest his spicy tidbit caused.

But Eric was not deceived. "You'd love to hear it. And no doubt you'll get the full details by sundown tomorrow." He grinned at her.

"Don't try to change the subject. Shani Moore doesn't seem to have much in common with you." Adeline walked with some effort to the den beckoning him to follow. She sat on a large sofa with huge stuffed pillows. A fire burned brightly in the brick fireplace.

"You mean her family background." Eric poured his mother a glass wine.

"I meant what I said. Thank you." She took a delicate sip of her one drink for the day. "Relationships are hard enough these days. It helps when you share the same views."

"We don't differ that much," Eric stared into the fireplace.

The yellow flames brought back the searing heat that had flashed through his body when he made love to Shani. She worked a kind of sorcery on his senses. Memories of her smile, the sound of her voice in his ear set his heart thumping and his mind reeling.

"My goodness. Things have gone that far then." Adeline clucked her tongue.

"What?" Eric started. He wiped perspiration from his upper lip with a handkerchief.

She gave him a wise smile. "It doesn't take a mind reader to know this Shani Moore has a special place in your heart. Just be careful. Opposites attract, but fights that electrify and stir passion early in a relationship can become bitter later on."

"That won't happen to us, Mama." Eric took her hand.

"Hello, hello. What this? Are you all right, darlin'?" Dalton sat next to his wife and peered at her with an anxious frown. "What's wrong, son?"

Adeline kissed her husband's cheek then wiped away her lipstick from it. "Nothing is wrong, Dalton. My, what a pair of worriers you are."

Dalton's shoulders relaxed. He grinned at his wife with affection. "Not me woman, I just want to know what you two are cooking up. What about a drink, son? Your mother won't object," he teased.

"No thanks, Dad. I've got to keep a clear head these days."

Adeline stood up. "That's my boy. Now y'all have to excuse me. I'm going to bed and watch a little television."

"I'll try not to disturb you when I finally turn in." Dalton said. He watched her walked away with a stiff gait. Seams of worry were etched into his face. "Your mother tries to hide just how bad she feels most of the time, Eric. I know it."

Eric pushed away his own fears. His voice had a forced heartiness even to his own ears. "Mama is doing much better. It's been over a year since she was in the hospital. Look how she's gotten back into the swing of her social life."

"Maybe you're right. Still, I'm going to get her to slow down some." Dalton turned an appraising eye on Eric. "Now what about you? Are you keeping a clear head?"

Eric lounged against the chair back. "Yep. I've been spending my days working on building coalitions and nights pouring over budget figures for three of the largest state departments. I don't intend to be caught off guard when the session begins."

"Good, do your home work. Don't let distractions trip you up, son. Or hormones rule your head." Dalton got up and went to the bar. He poured himself a glass of Chivas Regal.

Eric sat up straight. "What have my hormones got to do with anything?" A sinking feeling began in the pit of his stomach.

"Women are a gift, Eric. I'm the first to say so. But the wrong woman can be curse." Dalton waved his glass to punctuate his words.

"Dad, you're talking in riddles."

"I'm talking about that social worker you've been seen with lately. The one that's over...what's it called? Oh yeah, Mid-City Center. A lot of misguided social engineering that only helps people stay dependent." Dalton gave a grunt of disapproval.

"Dad, Mid-City has some very fine initiatives. And so what if I'm seeing Shani?"

Eric's jaw jutted out in a defensive expression that bordered on sullen. His father was making him feel like he was ten years old and had just broken a neighbor's window with his softball. Still, these were some of the same thoughts he'd had trying to convince himself not to get any closer to Shani. Now here he was defending the social programs his own party held in such low esteem. His conservative colleagues, Senator Raymond in particular, would not be pleased to say the least. It was obvious his father was thinking along the same lines.

"Son, you need to look to the future. I mean your future in politics, in the party. We need to establish credibility with men like Raymond." Dalton took a swig of his drink.

Eric spoke in a tight voice. "My record should more than speak for itself. The party doesn't rule my personal life."

"Listen, Eric, I understand." Dalton winked at him. "I was young and single once. Have your fun, boy. But don't advertise it."

Eric had a hard time checking his anger. He and his father had discussed his romantic escapades many times before. Yet this was very different. What he felt was different.

"Shani means a lot to me, Dad," he said speaking with measured deliberation.

Dalton eyed him steadily for several minutes. "I see. Then you need to rethink that, boy." He rose and put his now empty glass on the bar. "We've worked too hard to see it all unravel because you're infatuated."

Eric gripped the arm of the chair. "You mean you've worked too hard."

Dalton whirled to face him. "Damn right. For years being a conservative has gotten me scorn from the liberal black leaders; so-called leaders living off our community like parasites. And the white conservatives treated me like dirt, hell worse than dirt sometimes. But I held on to my principles and worked to build something for you. Don't throw it away for a little—"

Eric shot from his chair. "Don't say it, Dad." He turned his back to Dalton.

Dalton looked taken aback then contrite. "I'm sorry, son. I didn't mean to disrespect the young lady. But think of the consequences."

"My objectives haven't changed. Raymond knows that. I don't think anyone can question my commitment to the party platform." Eric took a deep breath and faced him. "My private life has nothing to do with it."

"Don't be naive, Eric. They're watching you like a hawk."

"Then I'll tell them exactly what I've just told you. Dad, Shani is a beautiful person. I want you to get to know her as a person, not a political label."

"Son, I'm sure she's a nice person..."

"I've invited her to our Christmas party at the club." Eric went to his father and put a hand on his arm. "Please, don't make this hard for us. Shani would really like to meet you and Mama. And it's important to me that you give her a chance."

After a long moment, Dalton covered Eric's hand with his own large one. "All right, son. I'll give it a try," was all he would venture. "But maybe an intimate dinner here just the four of us would be a more personal way to get acquainted first."

Eric brightened. "Hey, that's a great idea. Shani will be thrilled when I tell her. Thanks, Dad." He gave his father a rough embrace. "Well, I better get going. Lots of work to do."

"No problem, son. I'll see you later." Dalton smiled at him, but the smile faded when Eric turned away. His face became a rigid mask.

***

"And this is my office," Eric said sweeping a hand around. He wore a nervous smile. "The scene of the crime. What do you think?"

Shani stood between the door and his desk twisting the strap of her leather purse. She was not at ease either. Eric's last comment echoed her thought, making her wonder if it was written on her face. This is where plans were hatched to change the face of social service funding.

"Very nice," she replied with a smile. "Is your father here?" Shani resisted the urge to glance over her shoulder. Meeting Dalton Aucoin was the second cause of her discomfort.

"Oh, he's on a conference call with a couple of our satellite offices. He'll be here in a minute. Come on, honey, sit down. You look tired." Eric closed the door and fixed her a cup of coffee from the pot in his office.

Shani sat down. "You know how it is when you supervise a bunch of people. Why folks won't do right is a mystery to me." She shook her head then tasted the coffee. "Hey, your secretary makes great coffee."

"That is a sexist remark. Nedra didn't make it." Eric grinned at her expression of surprise.

"You mean ...?"

"Yep, Trumaine," Eric said with a laugh.

Shani gave his knee a playful swat. "Very funny."

"It's good to see you smile. You seemed really down all through lunch."

"Trying to rescue people from drugs seems like a losing battle some days. We can't seem to counter the call of street life." Shani closed her eyes and rubbed her temples.

"Baby, I'm sure you've gone to the limit trying to help them. So if you're beating yourself up thinking you could have done more, don't." Eric kissed her hand. "Mid-City is a lifeboat in a sea of troubles because of you."

"That's what worries me about the cuts, Eric. It's all about having the resources to give these kids choices. Jobs, help with tutoring, a mentor, or sometimes just a hand to hold can be lifesavers,"

Shani said.

"Eric, I have that report— Oh hello, Ms. Moore. Sorry, the door wasn't completely closed so I thought it was okay to come in." Despite his words, Trumaine entered the room with confidence.

Shani smothered the dislike that rose in her chest at the sight-of him for fear he would see it in her eyes. "Hello, Trumaine. How are you?"

"Fine. I won't take long, Eric. Nedra printed out this report and I've proofed it. Give me a call if you have any changes." Trumaine handed Eric a bound stack of papers.

"Great, Trumaine. Efficient as ever." Eric flipped through it before putting it on his desk.

Trumaine turned to Shani. "So how are things at Mid-City? Still running smoothly I hope."

"Routine. The same as with any organization. There are good days and bad." She felt foolish for being so paranoid.

"I heard that. Well, I'm on my way. Nice seeing you again. Senator, I'll meet with you at four, right?" Trumaine headed for the door.

"We're still on, Tru." Eric sat next to Shani again. "He's been a rock for me. A good assistant you can trust is worth his, or her, weight in gold."

"Amen. Elaine keeps me from losing my mind some days. Eric, about this dinner—"

"Sorry it took so long to get here." Dalton strode in. "So this is Ms. Shani Moore. Welcome to our little corner of the business world." He stepped back and studied her with an open, benevolent smile on his face.

Shani was caught off guard. "Pleased to meet you, Mr. Aucoin," she stammered.

"Call me Dalton, sugar."

He settled his large frame in a chair around a

coffee table in a corner of Eric's office. Eric and Shani sat on the small sofa.

"I'm so glad to finally meet you. Eric has been singing your praises to his mother and me. Thank you, son." Dalton accepted a large mug of coffee from him.

Shani flushed with pleasure. "It's a nice to meet you, too."

"Shani, Dad and Mom are both great cooks." Eric patted his father's knee with affection.

"And Adeline and I are looking forward to seeing you tomorrow night at dinner. You'll love Eric's mother. She's the sweetest woman in the world."

Shani shifted in her seat. "I'm looking forward to meeting her, too." But not being under a magnifying glass with two sets of critical eyes scouring out every little blemish.

"So Eric tells me you're a social worker." Dalton fixed his imposing gaze on her.

"Yes," Shani said. She shifted in her seat. "I'm at Mid-City Community Development, Inc."

"Doing some good things there I hear. Of course, some programs should put more responsibility on folks to pull themselves up out of poverty. The trouble with most of these social workers, no offense, honey, is they think money is the answer to everything. It's obvious all the liberal ways of tackling these problems haven't worked. I know you agree with me on that." Dalton gave a curt nod.

"Yes, well certainly mistakes have been made. We—" Shani began.

"Big mistakes, Shani." Dalton went on before she could finish. "The answer isn't to increased the money flow to what isn't working. We need a return to family values in the black community."

"Dad, Shani has some programs that stress just

those values. Tell him about the Teens Lending a Hand program, honey." Eric spoke up with animation.

"Well, yes. As a matter of fact—" Shani began.

Dalton's wrist watch alarm trilled a series of beeps. "Time for my next meeting. I'll be talking to Shreveport. What headaches I get just thinking about Louis and that crew. Goodbye, my dear. See you tomorrow night, kids." He bustled out after giving Shani a firm squeeze on the upper arm and Eric a clap on the back.

Shani inhaled and exhaled. "My goodness."

Eric chuckled. "Dad can be overwhelming at times."

"My head is spinning. He's a powerhouse." Shani gazed after the tall man.

"But he can be a real softie, too. Really." Eric laughed at the incredulous look she gave him.

"I hear he's faced down some of the toughest opponents, white and black, in this state to become successful in business. And he's not reluctant to tell some black leaders when he thinks they're wrong, which is often."

"But he will fight just as hard to right injustice or help someone in need. I can't wait for you two to get to know each other. And my mother, too. This is going to be the best holiday ever. My older sister, LeeAnne, is flying in a couple of days before Christmas." Eric put an arm around her.

Shani felt butterflies fluttering in her chest at the thought of being judged by yet another formidable member of the Aucoin clan. LeeAnne was senior vice president of retail sales for a large corporation. She lived in Atlanta with her husband and two children. One more appraising set of eyes to contend with in a few days.

"Yes, wonderful." Shani's voice was thin with

anxiety.

Eric pulled back to scan her face. "What's wrong? You sound less than enthusiastic. My family isn't that bad." He gave her chin a gentle pinch.

Shani bit her lip. She formed her words with care. "Eric, my family isn't like yours. Mama and Daddy worked hard to give us what we needed, but we very were poor. Brendon and I worked our way through college. And then there's J.J."

"Shani, I—"

"No, let me finish. My baby brother is in prison, Eric. He's serving a sentence on a drug charge." Shani let out a long breath.

"I know. Brendon is a computer analyst. His wife's name is Janine, they have two kids. J.J. has been in trouble since he was fourteen. I've known for a while now. And it's okay."

Shani went rigid. "Have you been investigating me or something? I'm not asking for your approval or begging you to excuse my family tree."

"That's not what I meant, Shani," Eric put in with a worried look.

"Well, it sure sounded like it. Furthermore, I don't like having a background check run on me by my dates." Shani pushed him away and stood up.

"Shani, wait a minute. You gave an interview to a newspaper reporter the day of the committee hearing. The reporter did a story on you and mentioned those things." Eric held out his hands in a gesture of conciliation. "Remember?"

Shani did remember the story. The story was supposed to be on the center but the reporter included information on her family as well. She felt a twinge of guilt for her fit of temper.

"I said a few things and the reporter did research. But I'm not ashamed of my family," she added in a defensive voice. "J.J. is going to turn his life around."

Eric took her in his arms again. "I'm sure he will. With you for a sister he's got a lot to be thankful for all ready. Did you really think so little of me? That I'd look down on J.J. and your parents?"

Shani was grateful to feel the hard arms around her. She rested against his chest. "I'm sorry, Eric. It's just that we've had to face a lot of folks passing judgment on us. Forgive me?" she murmured.

The scent cologne on his neck was glorious. Shani put her arms under his suit jacket around his body. Passion, warm and sweet, flowed from his hard body into hers.

"Baby, there's nothing to forgive. Now I better let you go before we set off the sprinkler system in here." Eric touched the tip of his tongue to the soft inside of her mouth for a second before letting her go. "Oh, man. How many hours until we meet tonight?"

Shani's legs were unsteady. "Too many. Now I'm going to have one heck of a time concentrating for the rest of the day. And this meeting with the city parish Human Services staff promises to be too dull for words."

"You can steel yourself for the ordeal while you drive the six blocks over there," Eric chuckled. "And I'll make it up to you tonight." He winked at her.

"I'm holding you to that." At least she could daydream about his embrace to get through what promised to be a drab afternoon of tedium.

***

"So what have you got, Trumaine?"

Dalton rocked back in the deep red leather captain's chair behind the massive, highly polished oak desk in his office. The picture window at his back over looked the street below and a small park. Dalton was proud of his office. For him it represented his triumph over all those who said he could not make it.

"Some very interesting information, sir. An ex-employee has given me evidence that could be quite helpful." Trumaine placed brown folder in front of Dalton. He leaned down to point at a paragraph. "Look at that."

"Interesting is right." Dalton balanced his bifocals on the end of his nose to read. "How widespread is this theft of goods from Mid-City."

"My source, frankly she's had her fingers stuck to property not hers, says it's the rule not the exception. And Ms. Moore has been ineffective in controlling it." Trumaine pressed his lips together.

"Ex-employee. Fired?"

Trumaine nodded. "Yes."

"Then she isn't credible. Happens all the time, they'll say. She's out for revenge because she got caught stealing." Dalton drummed his fingers on the blotter.

"There are indications that this has happened before, sir. And there's something else." Trumaine lifted the top page to show him the next one. "Involving Ms. Moore allowing a drug addict to remain on a payroll even though this addict has dropped out of the job training program."

"You mean Shani Moore is collecting the paycheck?" Dalton's head came up with a snap.

Trumaine gave a small sigh of disappointment. "Well not really, sir. The paycheck has been stopped, but under the guidelines, this M. Campbell should have been dropped from the list weeks ago. Bad management, pure and simple."

"It's not much, Trumaine. I'd hoped for more."

"I did the best I could with such a short time

frame, sir. Besides, with the proper handling a little can go a long way." Trumaine's lips twitched with the trace of a cunning grin.

Dalton looked at him with interest "How's that[1]"

"We don't have to prove anything. Just show inept management and questionable results for the money being spent" Trumaine lifted a shoulder. "The appearance of impropriety can be just as damaging. And the new conservative majority legislature won't need much convincing."

"You're right. With the rosy filter taken off his eyes, Eric should come back to his senses." Dalton swiveled his chair around to gaze out of the window. "He won't give up his career to support her when this comes out"

"Novelty, sir. I've been there myself a time or two." Trumaine let out a gruff laugh.

Dalton glanced at him sideways. "Yes I know." He suppressed a smile of satisfaction at the flash of worry that flittered across Trumaine's thin face for an instant "But how do we know the reporter will use it?"

"He was already doing a series on scandals involving funds mishandled by the Department of Health and Hospitals. I know the guy. He'll grab it like a dog goes after a juicy soup bone." Trumaine wore a smug look.

"Very good." Dalton let his gaze wandered around for a few seconds. The downtown buildings were decorated with garlands and red bows. "We need to get my son back on track. Hmm, it will come out when Eric wanted to introduce her to our social circle," he murmured to himself as though Trumaine was no longer in the room.

Trumaine wrinkled his long nose at the prospect "There would certainly be talk about that. Not to

mention how fast it would get back to Senator
Raymond."

Dalton did not answer or seem to notice
Trumaine was still present "Yes, the timing is just
right"

Chapter 5

"Come in, My'iesha." Shani held open the front door to the center.

Several other girls from the neighborhood had told her that My'iesha was pacing back and forth outside. Shani did not waste a minute. She did not want to miss an opportunity to connect with the skittish young woman again. My'iesha presented a tough exterior, gained from being bounced around ten foster homes by the time she was sixteen. She ran away at seventeen and was forced to do whatever she could to live. Though quick to insist she needed no one, her presence meant she was crying out for help. But she looked as though she might take flight.

"Please," Shani said.

My'iesha stood still, looking down the street instead of at Shani. "I can't stay long."

"Sure. Just a quick cup of coffee."

"All right I guess." My'iesha responded with a toss of her head. She sauntered past Shani. A childlike sketch of a Christmas tree topped with a gold star caught her eye. "Kids decorated. Hey, look at little Yusef's drawing. Pretty good for a seven-year-old," she said examining it.

"Yes, the children worked real hard on our decorations." Shani swept a hand around her. Not only were there drawings, but the children had hung garlands and made a two large wreaths for the double doors leading into the center. "They started right after Thanksgiving."

"Not bad." My'iesha did not move from the drawing. She stared at the signature.

"Yusef has asked about you several times," Shani said.

My'iesha's shoulders went rigid. "Yeah, well workin' in some after-school daycare is a pain."

"You volunteered to help out a couple of days a week after your part-time job. The kids loved your puppet shows."

"I ain't got time for none of that," My'iesha retorted in a tough girl voice.

Shani said nothing until they got to her office. When the door was closed, she poured hot water for the coffee. A few minutes later she handed her a cup. "This will take the chill off."

"Thanks." My'iesha took the mug and slumped into one of the chairs facing Shani's desk.

"So how've you been?"

"'Kay." My'iesha mumbled with her head down.

"Yusef isn't the only one who misses you. Maybe you could drop by sometime when Mrs. Martin is here. All the ladies in the senior citizens crafts class said to tell you hi."

My'iesha shifted in her seat. "What did you tell them? About me not being around anymore?"

"Just that you had a lot going on."

"Yeah, that's no lie," My'iesha said with a grunt. Silence stretched between them. "I guess you disgusted with me."

"I'm worried about you. Life is rough without friends." Shani sat next to her.

"You want me to come back?" My'iesha said in a little girl voice.

"Very much," Shani replied. She held her breath waiting.

"But how I'm gonna get my job back? You must have given it to somebody else by now." She relaxed a little.

"No, I kept it open for you."

My'iesha looked up at her with liquid eyes. "How

78

did you know I'd come back?"

"Because I know how much pride you took in doing a good job and how much it meant to you," Shani said with feeling.

"Well, maybe I can go by there next Tuesday." My'iesha plucked at a loose thread on the tight skirt she wore.

"Fantastic. I'll call them today. I'm glad you're back. My'iesha." Shani put her hand on My'iesha's shoulder. "We're going to be okay."

My'iesha could no longer stop the tears. She put down the cup and lay her head on Shani's shoulder.

***

"That was a wonderful meal, Mrs. Aucoin." Shani sat next to Eric in the large den.

She could not help but be impressed with her surroundings. The foyer of the spacious house was made festive with white lights strung around two tall potted trees. Fresh garlands draped over the windows of the formal living room and dining room, both decorated by professionals in ivory, green, and gold. The house smelled of a refreshing combination of pine and cinnamon. After dinner, Mrs. Aucoin had insisted they be informal and relax in the den.

"Now let's have Dalton fix us a drink. He just loves playing bartender," Adeline winked at her.

"And I'm good if I do say so myself." Dalton called out from behind the bar. "Here we go. Chardonnay for you, sweetheart. Ginger ale for my son who's driving, and brandy for his lady." He sat on the wide arm of the chair Adeline occupied with a glass of bourbon for himself. "So Shani, you're from Baton Rouge?"

"Actually I was born in Evangeline Parish, but my parents moved to Baton Rouge when I was a baby." Shani took a sip of the brandy.

"And you have a master's degree. What school?" Dalton kept his tone casual.

"Undergraduate at Southern, master's at LSU." Shani cleared her throat. This was the part of the evening she'd dreaded. Soon Mrs. Aucoin would jump in with questions of her own.

"I understand you have two brothers. What do they do?"

"Dad—" Eric cut in before Shani could speak. He frowned at Dalton.

"No, Eric. It's okay. My older brother, Brendon, is a computer analyst. My youngest brother, J.J., is in prison."

Dalton's expression showed no surprise. "I see." He glanced at Eric then Adeline. "How unfortunate."

"Both my parents are dead. They were poor, working people. My mother finished high school. My father never did. I don't have any educated, well-to-do relatives or a fancy family history." Shani spoke in an even tone without hostility, a tone that said "take it or leave it."

Adeline's handsome features clouded over. "Dalton, you should be ashamed. You sound like a police officer questioning a suspect." She faced Shani. "Excuse my husband, Shani. He can be hard to take sometimes."

Dalton waved away his wife's admonishment. "What's everybody getting so upset about? I was just making conversation. Getting acquainted."

Shani scanned his face. "Is there something else you want to know, Mr. Aucoin? A lot of people are curious about my younger brother. It's natural."

She was used to the questions and shocked

whispers behind her back. It was obvious Mr. Aucoin wanted to see if she would mention J.J. being in prison. And he wanted Eric and his wife to hear it.

"That's quite enough, Dalton," Adeline said in a sharp voice. "Shani, this is our first meeting and we know quite enough for now. I don't believe in spilling family secrets to those you barely know." She smiled at Shani with genuine fondness. "But I do hope we will become closer."

"Thank you, Mrs. Aucoin. I'd like that."

Shani was so touched, tears came to her eyes. She took a deep breath and blinked them back. Adeline's warm, maternal personality reminded her of how much she missed her mother.

"My son looks at you the way I've never seen him look at another young woman. I have a feeling we'll be seeing more of each other." The twinkle in Adeline's eyes returned.

"Mama, please," Eric said with an embarrassed expression.

Dalton glanced at his wife and son. His stern expression relaxed. "Sure, there will be plenty of time for spilling family secrets. Hell, we've got more than a few Aucoins who've been in jail. My wife's family couldn't keep their hands off other folks' livestock." He guffawed.

"Dad! That was almost eighty years ago." Eric's troubled look shifted to one of relief. He gripped Shani's hand to reassure her.

Adeline laughed. "More recent than that, sweetie. Now, what about Christmas? Shani, you must join us."

For the next few hours the conversation moved from making plans for the holidays to sports. To Shani's surprise, she did not feel as though the talk was forced or superficial. Could she fit into Eric's life? Of course, J.J.'s crime was more serious than cattle theft. Would Adeline still be so understanding when she learned he had been a drug dealer? She felt a growing affection for the kind, gentle woman who seemed so different from her husband. Dalton Aucoin. Shani doubted there was little he did not know about her all ready. Yet he had never treated her with anything but a courtly kind of old fashion courtesy. Maybe her fears were unfounded. Finally the evening ended.

Back at her apartment, Shani poured them each a cup of hot herbal tea. "This will help us sleep."

Eric frowned at the steaming brew. "Not what I had in mind." He ducked her playful swat with a chuckle. "Just joking. I've got an early day tomorrow. I'd better drink this and go. It's eleven all ready."

"Yeah, I need to get a fresh start myself. I've got back- to-back meetings all day." Shani settled onto the sofa near him. "So do you think tonight went okay?"

Eric put down his cup. "Honey, it went really well. Dad's opinionated, pushy sometimes, and a bit of a snob, but he's a good person at heart. Honestly, I thought he'd be worse." He grinned.

"Hey, it's normal that your father would want to know. He cares about you and your career. Who you associate with can ruin your career as a politician." Shani bit her lower lip. She had been a fool not to have realized it before now. Dalton's questions hit home with the force of dynamite. Those same questions would be asked by others. The answers could be weapons used against Eric.

"My constituents are not that narrow-minded." Eric moved close to her. "So don't worry about my career."

"But you might have lots of problems because of me." Shani let out a sigh of dismay.

"And we'll handle them. Together," he said in a soft voice.

"But—"

Eric silenced her with a kiss. Shani melded her body to his, anxiety dissolved at the touch of his tongue to hers. "Eric, this is serious," she mumbled. Her breath quickened with each brush of lips brushed against her neck. His hands moved up her thighs to her breasts.

"Baby, you can't tell how serious I am?" he whispered. "I want you, Shani. And nothing will come between us. Nothing."

In a soft haze of desire, they found their way to her bed. They lay together naked within minutes of frantic undressing. Once again his strong body moved with hers in a rhythmic dance of passion. He moved with enough speed to lift her close to the edge of ecstasy, then slowed leaving her crying for more. And more he gave. Shani trembled at the delicious torture of delay.

"Eric," Shani moaned.

Over and over she said his name, her voice rising with the strength of each thrust His cries told her he would delay no longer. First Shani came, a shower of bright colors exploding in her head. Eric groaned holding her tight as he shuddered inside her. They went limp in each other's arms, gasping for breath. For a long time neither spoke. They enjoyed holding each other. Eric combed his fingers through Shani's thick hair while she pressed her cheek to his broad chest.

"Now isn't this better than any old herbal tea?" Eric's chest rumbled with mirth.

Shani giggled. "You got that right."

"And I don't want you worrying about my career. Even if it did make a difference, which it won't, I couldn't give you up now. I love you too much." Eric lifted her chin to gaze into Shani's eyes.

"I love you, too. I love you like crazy." Shani kissed him long and hard.

***

Terrilyn came into the living room of her spacious town- house carrying a huge bowl of popcorn. "I saw Robert the other day. Claudia dumped him."

"Ah, too bad," Shani said in a voice heavy with sarcasm.

"He asked about you. Honey, he wants you back bad. It was written all over his pitiful face. Go girl. Two fine men after you is *good* for the ego."

"You called Robert a low down, no good mongrel. Now you sound like he's the catch of the day." Shani stared at her friend in mock outrage.

"He's a dog to his heart, girl. No question. But he's a fine dog with money." Terrilyn popped a kernel into her mouth.

The two women were dateless, Eric was working late, and Terrilyn's latest flame was working a night shift. So they decided to spend Friday night watching movies and eating snacks to console themselves. They sat on Terrilyn's sofa bed that she bought for when her mother or one of her sisters came from Shreveport to visit. Propped against oversized pillows, they were snug and ready to cry over their favorite movie, Black Orpheus.

"Having Robert slither back does nothing for my ego, Terrilyn. He doesn't care about me." Shani arranged the heavy cotton throw over her legs.

"Even better. Honey, rub that wound raw. Let the little mangy puppy do a slow burn thinking about some other man giving you good love."

The corners of Shani's mouth turned up with the trace of a grin. "You're wicked. Darn, this video is acting strange."

"Surprise, surprise. We've played the thing a zillion times. Maybe it's worn out." Terrilyn tried to help clear the picture by pressing buttons on the remote.

"Or maybe you should invest in a new DVD player. They delivered this one in a horse and buggy." Shani dodged a pillow.

"Look. I give up. But have no doubt I'm going to buy a new copy of this classic. Let's see what's on the movie channel." Terrilyn turned to a local station and was about to switch when Shani stopped her.

"Wait, it's the ten o'clock news."

"Who cares? Look, the television guide says The Color Purple is on Channel thirty-two starting . . . now. I could watch that movie another dozen times at least, girl."

Shani grabbed the remote from her. "No you don't. There's Eric." She pointed to the screen.

"Who is that cutie next to him? Oh, I love those soulful eyes." Terrilyn leered.

"Trumaine Delacrosse, Eric's aide. Now will you hush?"

"Senator Raymond and a group of freshman legislators have mapped out a plan to address the serious fiscal problems of this state." A black female reporter spoke into the camera before the picture switched back to the group of about fifteen men who stood in the lobby of the state capitol building in downtown Baton Rouge.

Senator Raymond, with thick gray hair and a puffy face, stood at a podium with microphones positioned in front of him. "We believe that a drastic change in the way we do business in state government is necessary. No longer can will we allow those who will not work to live off the sweat of hard-working, decent men and women. Our message to them is simple, the party's over."

All fifteen of the men, including Eric, applauded his words.

The female reporter came back on camera. "Among the areas targeted for reduction are block grants to several community centers where there has been evidence of poor administration or misapplication of funds. According to Senator Raymond, details will soon follow. This is Cynthia Bienville for Channel two."

Shani and Terrilyn sat silently for several seconds.

Terrilyn finally broke the tense quiet. "I can see those wheels of suspicion turning. Don't jump to conclusions."

"But did you see him cheerleading that old bag of wind? What am I supposed to think?" Shani wanted to cry. "Maybe Eric is a liar and just using me."

Terrilyn turned down the sound of the television. "You told me that Eric never claimed to be a converted liberal after you two got together. But he did promise to consider input from you and other social workers."

Shani chewed a finger and stared at the picture of a weather map. "How can I be sure he'll stick by that when he's faced with all his party members?"

"He's only one man, Shani. He can't change everyone or do it alone. He can only try." Terrilyn shrugged.

Shani felt better as she digested her words. "As usual you're brilliant."

"You just figured that out?" Terrilyn quipped.

"Let's get another round of drinks before we get into Whoopi's premier performance." She padded into the kitchen in her bunny slippers.

"You're absolutely right. I'm being so childish. Of course, Eric will be outnumbered when it comes to defending agencies like Mid-City. But he can make a difference." Shani smiled at the strawberry flavored soft drink Terrilyn handed her. "My favorite."

"Hey, nothing but the best for our slumber party. And for me, old fashioned Barq's root beer. Now, here's to Senator Aucoin. A man for all seasons." Terrilyn raised a clear mug filled to the top.

"To Senator Aucoin. A man after my own heart." Shani clinked her glass against the mug.

"He's after more than that, honey. And count your lucky stars for it." Terrilyn winked at her.

"Every day, sugar. Every fun-filled day." Shani snickered with her. They spent the rest of the night watching movies and talking about everything under the sun.

Chapter 6

Only six days until Christmas. What a difference a few weeks made. Shani sang along with the carolers grouped in front of a huge, elaborately decorated tree in the middle of the mall. Unlike her previous shopping trips, the festive mood made the task easy. Enjoyable even. She glanced at her watch and hurried to the next store. The smell of leather drew her toward a row of briefcases and portfolios. There it was, a leather bound journal. Though a modern man, Eric still loved old books and writing notes by hand, like his to-do list. Perfect for a busy senator, Shani mused feeling a flush of happiness at the thought of giving it to Eric.

She whizzed through the rest of mall picking up items for everyone on her list. The only time her mood darkened was when she picked out a MP3 player for J.J. Another Christmas separated from him. And this year would be even worse when she went to visit him Sunday without Brendon. Yet she could not stay sad for long. A glance at the bright green holiday shopping bag, Eric's wrapped gift nestled in among the rest of her treasures, lifted her up again. Somehow she would make things right between her brothers. This Christmas was filled with hope and a kind of newness.

Back at the office, Shani dove into the pile of messages on her desk with gusto. Elaine chattered away through the open door as she worked about her plans for the holidays.

"Yeah, honey. I can't wait. I've been saving up all year for my new sound system. Me and Wayne gonna celebrate pushing the last of our kids out of the nest by throwing the best darn New Year's Eve groove fest in this old town." Elaine snapped her fingers to the beat of Otis Redding singing "Merry Christmas, Baby" coming from the radio on her desk.

"Sounds good to me." Shani laughed.

"Yep. You and Senator Aucoin are coming, right'"

"Yes indeed. When I told Eric, he grinned from ear to ear. We'll hit your place first then go to the big ball down at the Radisson. It's going to be one stupendous beginning to the New Year," Shani murmured.

"I heard that." Elaine gave a low chuckle.

Shani's eyes widened in embarrassment. Shani hadn't realized she'd spoken aloud. "I mean . . .," she stammered to find the right words.

Elaine glanced up at her when she came out carrying signed memos and letters. "You mean great parties are always nice." She wore a knowing grin.

"Yes, they are." Shani went back into her office smiling. She tapped out a beat on her desk. "Bringin' all them good ole presents for my baby an' me, ha-ha-ha," she sang along with the gravel voiced soul music legend.

"Merry Christmas, baby." Elaine took up the song. "You sho did treat me nice."

They both dissolved into giggles. Suddenly Elaine's voice was cut off by the ring of the telephone.

"Merry Christmas, Mid-City Center. How may I help you? Yes she's in." Elaine put the call through. "Senator Hot Chocolate on line two."

Shani was still laughing when she pushed the button. "Hello, Eric. Yes I know you're working late tonight."

"Now don't be that way. You know how it is." Eric's voice was soft and placating.

"But it's almost Christmas. I'll bet none of those other lawmakers are putting in overtime like this.

Typical Type A behavior."

"We've made a lot of headway with our proposals. And I'm wrapping up the last of a few loose ends now. We're ready to bring this state back to fiscal responsibility." Eric switched back to his businesslike tone.

Shani cradled the phone and shuffled a stack of papers. "Save it for the news conference, mister," she teased. "What about tonight? Or must I languish in loneliness once more?"

"Take heart, lovely one. I'll be all yours in a few short hours."

"Can't wait."

"Bye, love." Eric's voice went low and sensuous.

"Bye, honey." Shani sighed and sank against the back of her chair. She stared up at the ceiling.

"Can I come in?" Paulette stood in the door.

"Sure. Get some coffee."

"In a minute. Have you read today's paper?"

"No. Yesterday's either. I've been wrapping gifts and trying to get the last of these presents. Cortana Mall opened at seven this morning. A lot of stores had early bird pre-Christmas sales, and it was wild." Shani's bright mood faded when she noticed Paulette's expression. "What's wrong?"

Paulette's face was taut with anger. She slapped a newspaper down on Shani's desk. "Look at that."

Shani read aloud. "Theft Widespread at Local Help Centers." The headline was bad enough but it got worse. "Conservative senate investigation spearheaded out of—" Shani broke off for several seconds as a sick feeling began through her midsection. "Out of freshman Senator Aucoin's office supports the need for changes in the way some social programs are administered."

"It seems Senator Aucoin used his visits to build a

case against us." Paulette pressed her lips together. She moved with short jerky motions filling a mug with black coffee. She thumped down the container of creamer. "Of all people, he takes the word of a woman who is a known liar."

Shani's heart pounded as she read the article silently. The thin sheets slipped from her fingers when she was done. "There must be a reason for this."

"Hell yes there's a reason!" Paulette blurted. "Senator Raymond and his minions want to shut us down."

"No, Paulette. Eric told me he wouldn't..."

Her voice trailed off because she remembered his words. Eric had never promised he would protect the programs if there was evidence of poor management. But he must see that this so-called evidence did not come from a credible source. Shani stared out the window at the weathered, wood frame homes just across the street. A child no more than two years old played in the dirt with two older children. All three wore ragged, thin sweaters. Had she been so blinded by emotion that she'd given Eric the ammunition needed by his conservative party leaders? Shani closed her eyes to stop the tears pushing to form.

"Shani, these guys have all the conviction of religious zealots when it comes to social programs. Or social engineering as they call it." Paulette glanced at Shani. When she spoke her tone was sympathetic. "Maybe Eric didn't know the information he had about Mid-City would be twisted to show us in the worse possible light."

Shani turned from the window to look her in the eyes. "You don't believe that and neither do I. Eric is very practical and no dummy."

"Eric isn't quoted in this article." Paulette picked

up the newspaper and scanned the article again. She had the posture of someone grasping at straws. "His aide Trumaine Delacrosse gave a statement that the inquiry is continuing."

"Eric knows everything that goes on in his office, Paulette." Shani's anguish hardened into to fury.

"I've worked for other people and run my own private practice. It's very possible not to know everything your employees are doing. It was months later that I found letters one of my former secretaries was supposed to have sent out. I wanted to call her up and fire her again." Paulette leaned forward in her chair. "All I'm saying is, give him a chance to explain."

Shani squinted at her. "Why are you defending him? I know how you feel about black conservatives."

Paulette sank back against the chair. "And I know finding that special person doesn't happen very often. Two years ago, I broke it off with Reginald. I thought he was too rigid and conservative. You know what? He's married to a woman who makes me look like a right-wing reactionary. They have a beautiful baby girl."

"This is more than a difference in political views now. Eric may have used me, lied to me, to further his political career and impress Senator Raymond." Shani could not keep her voice from wavering.

Paulette stood up to go. "I won't try and dress it up, sugar. This looks pretty bad," she said pointing to the newspaper. "Make him explain. Bring him to his knees to beg forgiveness and swear to make it right. But don't be too quick to write him off."

Shani accepted her quick goodbye hug, and closed up in her office after Paulette left. She tried to call Eric. His secretary told her he was gone to an afternoon meeting. Fruitless hours of trying to concentrate on the new five-year plan, memos to staff, and the quarterly budget report left her spent. A tap on the door made her glance up from the rows of figures on a spreadsheet.

"Yes? Oh, Elaine." Shani rubbed her tired eyes.

"Have a good evening. I'm going home now."

"It's five already?" Shani glanced at the clock on her credenza. She was shocked at how time had passed. In one hour, Eric would be at her apartment.

"Yeah, and my husband is probably burning up chicken even as we speak. His night to cook," Elaine said with a laugh. Her laughter died when she saw the gloom on Shani's face. "Listen, I know it's none of my business but... Give Senator Aucoin a chance to explain."

"Oh, you can bet I want him to tell me all about this one," Shani shot back.

Elaine came into the room and sat opposite her. "I mean, take time to hear what he's saying. You still may not agree, but listen without judgment. My mama taught me that not long after I got married. Her and Daddy were together forty-two years."

"Thanks, Elaine. I'll try to remember that." Shani tried to lift the corners of her mouth into a smile and only half succeeded.

"Good night." Elaine hesitated at the door. "And take care."

"Bye."

Shani was touched by Elaine's concern. She was both anxious and reluctant to see Eric. Part of her was poised to demand answers, another part wanted to avoid what promised to be a painful confrontation. As she changed clothes, she tried to follow Elaine and Paulette's advice.

"I'll keep calm and ask him about the article. Let him talk without interrupting," she said the words trying to make her outrage subside. She glanced at herself in the full length mirror on the bedroom closet door. "After all, there could be a reasonable explanation." The woman staring back at her looked far from convinced. At that moment, the double chimes of her doorbell sounded.

Shani took a deep breath and opened the door. "Hi.

How've you been?" She resisted the urge to avoid the kiss on her forehead.

"Whew! What a grueling day. But knowing I'd end it with you made it bearable. Sorry I'm late. But the meeting went on way past the one hour they promised. Then I ran by the house to change." He took off his leather jacket to reveal a forest green sweater, striped cotton shirt underneath, and dark brown pants. "I was tired of wearing that suit and tie."

"Oh, I see." Shani sat next to him, her back straight.

Eric crossed an ankle over one knee. "So how's my sweetie doing? Your day was better than mine I hope." He dropped a muscular arm behind her on the sofa's back.

"It started out okay. Then it went downhill real fast. But of course you know about it." She shot him an accusing glance. His casual behavior was infuriating. Did he think his charms were so over powering she would forgive anything?

"I do?"

"Yes, since you saw fit to trash my reputation in the Advocate. "Shani picked up the newspaper from her coffee table and waved it.

"What? Oh, the article about problems at help centers. Baby, I told you we would be looking into them. And—"

"But did you ask for reactions from us?" Shani's

ire sprang forward like a hot spark. "You planned this all along. I should have seen it coming."

"Now hold on, I didn't trash your reputation." Eric spoke in an unruffled tone. "Trumaine described problems in his report identified long ago. Some of them you and other directors pointed out."

"Widespread theft common at the agencies? I don't recall ever saying that. How could you listen to the allegations of one disgruntled ex-employee and splash it all over the wire service?" Shani glared at him.

"What?" Eric took the paper from her hand. A frown creased his face as he saw the headline. "I didn't see this edition. I've been swamped and Trumaine only gave me a summary of major stories, including this one. This isn't the way it was supposed to be done."

"What do you take me for? You want to destroy our credibility so we won't have any chance to get funding." Shani turned her face from him. "You're good, I have to give you credit."

"What does that mean?" Eric's jaw clenched.

"It means you used your oily charm to dazzle me. You knew all the right words to lull me into trusting you. How you cared about the poor but wanted the money to be used wisely. Self-determination is what our community needs. But that's not the best part. No, your most impressive performances were when you said how special I was to you," Shani said in a hoarse voice. "And now you think I'm so in love I'll accept any thin lie you offer me?"

"Honey, that's not true at all! Shani, you have to believe me." Eric clutched her arm. "I didn't know the reports of theft would be made the focus by this reporter. Even more important, I never lied about my feelings for you."

Shani twisted from his grasp. "I tried to convince myself all afternoon you couldn't have known about it. But this sentence kept ringing in my head." She jabbed a finger at the last paragraph. "According to Senator Aucoin, these programs are aimed at keeping the poor dependent and provide jobs for social workers. I've heard you say that at least a half dozen times."

"And it's what I believe." Eric drew himself up to his full height. "Look, if these programs can stand up to scrutiny then you've got nothing to worry about. But I resent being accused like this. You always knew my views."

"So you admit being behind this?" Shani was flabbergasted despite her early suspicions. What brass to show such arrogance. How could she have misjudged him so much?

"Shani, you knew all along all of the budget items were under a microscope." Eric's face was like a gathering storm of thunder and lightning. "I think we'd better both stop before we say things that can't be taken back."

Shani stared at him coldly. "I wonder just how far you'd go to get ahead politically. What with Congressman Johnson announcing he won't run for the House of Representatives next election. Your name has been mentioned more than once." She remembered a speech in which Eric talked about his ambition to run for Congress one day.

Eric looked at her through narrowed eyes that glinted with indignation. "And you're willing to defend programs that waste the taxpayers' money even when it's obvious every dollar must count in the black community. Save the status quo no matter what. Is that it?"

"So you don't bother to deny your agreement

with this hatchet job of an article," Shani spat at him. "I should have known."

Eric picked up his jacket. "Maybe we haven't known each other long in terms of time, but I thought you knew what kind of person I am." He walked to the door. "Obviously I was wrong."

Shani felt a warm flow down her cheek and tasted salt. She turned from him. "You counted on using the famous Eric Aucoin charisma. Didn't work this time, pal. That's what you were wrong about." She made her voice hard as steel.

"If that's the way you see it fine. Good thing I found out early in the game. Who needs this?"

When the door slammed behind him, Shani felt the jolt more than on a physical level. She collapsed onto the sofa and gave in to the urge to weep. A tidal wave of loss washed over her that left her feeling weak and more lonely than she had since losing her mother.

***

Brendon's fine black brows drew together over chocolate brown eyes. "You sick? Looks like you haven't slept in weeks." He paused in wrapping gifts for Colin and Kara.

He and Janine used Shani's apartment as a hiding place for their Christmas toys. With Christmas only two days away, they did the usual. Ate dinner out then came over to get everything that needed assembling put together.

Janine slapped his arm. "Nice going, Brendon. Make her feel even better by telling her she looks awful," she muttered.

Shani came back into the living room with three cups of hot cocoa. She managed a feeble smile. "It's okay, Janine. He's never been one for diplomacy."

Brendon ignored his wife's reproof. "Shani, what's wrong? You know better than to try and hide anything from me. I can look at you in two seconds and see something bad has happened."

"It's just..." Shani bit her bottom lip unable to go on.

His eyes went wide with fear. "Is it J.J.? Did he get hurt in prison? You don't want to tell me because of the way I've been acting, is that it?"

"No, no," Shani said in a rush to calm his rising panic. "J.J. is doing fine. This has nothing to do with him."

Brendon let out a long, slow breath. His relief was visible as he clasped Janine's hand on his arm. "Then what? Work got you down? I've told you about running yourself ragged at that center. Why you don't go into private practice with this psychiatrist friend of mine is beyond me."

Janine shook her head at him. "Brendon, you sure can miss the boat sometimes."

"I don't know what you mean. If it's one thing I understand, it's my baby sister. She's got herself all worked up about a misguided kid or poor welfare mother with no more food stamps." Brendon went back to wrapping a doll for Kara. "You've got to learn some day not to take all the world's problems on your shoulders. You'll wind up with an ulcer."

"Wrong again, Mr. Perceptive. Shani, I read that article." Janine wore a sympathetic expression.

"What article?" Shani busied herself tying a ribbon.

"The one that has probably caused big trouble between you and Eric Aucoin," Janine said.

"Shani and Senator Aucoin?" Brendon blinked as though waking up from a nap.

"Brendon, I mentioned it to you several times. You said, 'That's nice, baby.'" Janine turned to Shani. "He's been up to his neck in work for weeks."

"Yeah, I remember something about Shani having a date. But with Senator Aucoin? He's a staunch conservative." Brendon gazed at his sister in amazement.

Janine gave a short laugh and pointed him to the extra bedroom Shani used as an office where other toys still waited to be wrapped. "Here, sweetie. Put this pin ball machine together. I'll catch you up later."

Brendon took the large game from her. "Don't be such a smart aleck. And I'm not going anywhere. Besides, I saw the article you're talking about, and now I do remember about Shani and Senator Aucoin." He seemed close to sticking his tongue out at her.

"Lord, I'm so humiliated. Why don't we just rent a billboard that says 'Shani Moore, proof that you can be the same kind of fool *twice*.'" Shani spoke in an acrid voice.

"Oh, come on. You knew the guy's politics when you met him. At least he was always honest. Something you can't say about a lot of public officials. In fact, I have to agree with some of what he says—" Brendon held up a finger in preparation of launching a discourse.

"Honey, please," Janine cut in. "Shani, from the look on your face, I'd say you had one mean argument with him. Right?"

"It was awful. I got angry, one word led to another, and well you know." Shani pushed aside the green shiny paper in her lap.

"Too awful for reconciliation?" Janine put an arm around her shoulders.

"It's not just an argument. He used our relationship to get information against Mid-City. And not only could we be hurt. Every center in this state might suffer."

"Are you sure his party or maybe another legislator didn't use his name to avoid being called racists? They do stuff like that you know. Don't be too quick to think he's a bum." Brendon wore a self-satisfied expression at the surprise his comment brought. "Pretty perceptive of me, huh? I haven't been that immersed in work."

"Amazingly, he could be right." Janine rubbed her chin in thought. "What did Eric say about the article?"

"He claimed not to have known they would go the sensational route and use that theft allegation." Shani kicked a wad of paper across the carpet. "Either way, he's being used. And had the nerve to get an attitude with me."

"I guess so if you jumped the brother," Brendon snorted. "I'd catch a 'tude myself if you called me a liar to my face."

Janine sent him a scathing glance. "What my husband must mean is harsh words lead to hard feelings. But if he wasn't guilty, he should have just answered the questions."

"Excuse me, I know what I meant. Look, Shani, I know how strongly you feel about those programs. Maybe you didn't give the guy much of a chance to tell his side. Maybe the man just made a mistake."

"Eric Aucoin didn't make a mistake. I'm sure of it. Now the subject is closed," Shani said in a firm voice.

"Okay. If you say so." Brendon cocked an eyebrow at his wife.

"And don't give any eye signals behind my back either." Her foot bumped against a gift bag under her small Christmas tree. One of J.J.'s gifts, homemade tea cakes from her grandmother's recipe. "Besides, you don't practice what you preach." Shani pointed a finger at his nose.

"Meaning?"

"Meaning J.J. has very little to look forward to during Christmas except visits from us. Why can't you forgive him?" Shani shoved thoughts of Eric away to focus on a different source of pain.

"It's not the same. J.J. hurt Mama with his wild behavior. And his being in prison is a disrespect to her and Daddy's memory." Brendon had a stubborn set to his square jaw.

"He's ashamed of himself, Brendon. He needs us to stand by him." Shani wanted to shake reason into him.

Janine looped her arm through his. "Sweetheart, we both know how torn up you're going to be if you don't see him. You're miserable," she said to him in a soft voice.

"J.J. is not going to put my entire family in prison with him. He made his choices. Now let him deal with the consequences. Let's drop it." Brendon stormed out of the room.

Janine nodded to Shani. "Talk to him alone. This is something only you can help him work through."

Shani followed him into her office. She pushed aside empty boxes that only recently held toys and other gifts now wrapped. "Brendon, I know you feel partly responsible for J.J., but it's not your fault. He *did* make certain choices."

Brendon stood with his back to her staring out the window into the night "I was so into high school, the band, and Charlene. Or was it Darlene?" He gave a grunt of self- disgust. "I can't even remember her name. J.J. was drifting from mischief into crime while I went to parties and hung out with my buddies. Oh, I remembered my promise to Daddy. I lied to myself that a few lectures and taking him to the movies once in a while was the best I could do."

Shani stepped closer to him. "You were only a teenager yourself. I counsel parents much older than you were at the time who can't figure out how to save their kids from the streets. It really isn't your fault, Brendon."

He turned to her, his face drawn with torment. "You don't think I failed you both?"

Shani hugged him to her. "*No*. J.J. and I looked up to you. We always thought we'd never be able to be half the person you are today. J.J. understands your anger. He doesn't think he's worthy of you."

"Mama used to clap her hands and laugh with joy seeing us running to get our presents Christmas mornings. She would say . . ." Brendon could not go on.

"She'd say, 'Ain't nothin' like bein' with family on Christmas. Thank you, Jesus. I can feel your daddy smilin' down on us, too,' " Shani finished for him. "Please, come with me Sunday."

Brendon wiped his eyes. "Here are his presents." He pointed to a large bag. He wore a sheepish expression, "We went overboard and spoiled him as usual."

"Now you can give them to him yourself. By the way, he agrees you shouldn't bring the children." Shani squeezed his hand.

"Thanks little sister." Brendon shook off his somber mood. "Now quit stalling. You suggested I buy this contraption, and you're going to help me put it together." He held up a wide sheet of instructions with tiny print.

"My goodness! We're going to be here all night."

For the next hour, the three of them wrestled to finish. Shani was relieved to the see tension melt from her older brother. He laughed with ease as though a weight was lifted from his shoulders. The holiday would not be so bad after all. Then she thought of Eric. The bright lights and shiny wrapping seemed to go dim. She continued to chatter with them, but her heart was not in it.

"Bye, sis. See you Sunday," Brendon said. He kissed her forehead.

"Take all this stuff and put it in the trunk, babe. I'm coming." Janine loaded his arms with tools and bags. "Thanks for everything, sugar."

"Hey, you don't have to thank me. I love wrapping presents for our beautiful babies."

"I'm not talking about that. Thanks for helping Brendon unload that heartache he's been lugging around for months." Janine hugged and kissed her. "About Eric Aucoin, from what I hear he's a good person."

"Janine, I just don't know what to think."

"Try to work it out once more. No accusations, just openly share the hurt you feel. Talk to him."

"It's not so simple." Shani hugged herself against the cold that came from inside, not the chill night air.

Janine sighed. "Honey, it never is. But from the light in your eyes when you talked about him, I'd say don't give up without a fight. Promise you'll consider what I've said?"

Shani said nothing but nodded in response. Alone, she faced the bleak truth. There was no way to bridge the gulf between her and Eric. He had taken advantage of her. Maybe planned it from the beginning. No, it was over. A least this time she hadn't spent years being deceived. And she had survived last New Year's Eve without someone special to hold at midnight. She would make it through to the dawning of another new year as well.

***

"Come in, Trumaine," Eric said in a clipped tone. He drummed his fingers on his desk. For the last twenty-four hours he'd simmered, unable to confront him. Trumaine had taken the previous day off. "I left messages on your answering machine."

"I spent the night in New Orleans with a friend after we finished shopping at the River Walk. You ready for Christmas?" Trumaine strolled in and poured himself a cup of coffee.

Eric ignored his question. "Tell me about this article." He held up the newspaper.

"Which article is that?" Trumaine took a sip from the cup. He squinted at the fine print.

"The one 'spearheaded out of my office,'" Eric snapped. "The one that implies Shani Moore and several community center directors are incompetent at best and thieves at worst. The article you summarized for me the other day. You left out a few rather important details."

"You and I discussed gathering information for our reports to Senator Raymond. But I told you there were problems at those agencies. I provided that information to Senator Raymond's office as we agreed."

"But you decided what information to send. An allegation made by an angry woman fired from her job is not the basis to make judgments about an entire organization," Eric said, his voice rising.

"Senator Raymond specifically asked for a complete report and I gave it to him. It was their decision to use the reports of pilfering."

"I see," Eric said.

"In more than one instance, programs were being mismanaged." Trumaine lifted his chin. "I thought the purpose of our investigation was to expose these abuses."

"But based on credible evidence. Not hearsay and unconfirmed rumors. And definitely not from such a suspect source as some woman fired when she was caught stealing," Eric said.

"Senator Raymond—"

"Senator Raymond doesn't run my office," Eric cut him off. He stood up and planted both fists on the desk top. "You listen to me, and listen to me good. I decide what goes out of this office to Senator Raymond or any of the party leaders. Frankly, I think you knew damn well how that information would be put to use."

Trumaine faced him with a cool expression. "He expected to get very specific information. Of course, I understand your relationship with Ms. Moore is at a delicate stage. But so is your political career. It's in your best interest to *cooperate* with Senator Raymond."

"My relationship with Ms. Moore is none of your business." Eric spoke with such heat that Trumaine's cool exterior faltered for a split second. "And as for Senator Raymond, I won't jump when he speaks just to advance my political career. Apparently you have your own career ambitions in mind."

Trumaine paused before he spoke. "Senator Raymond is a powerful man in this state."

"And known for rewarding loyalty." Eric had a sour taste in his mouth.

"Bucking men like Raymond is political suicide. And I intend a steady rise up the food chain. I thought you had the same plans. Until now." Trumaine's lips curled with a hint of derision.

Eric crossed his arms. "Oh I'll be moving up. But not with my lips planted firmly on anyone's rear end.

And if Senator Raymond expects that, then *he* can go jump."

Trumaine raised both eyebrows. "You want to be careful with that kind of talk or you could find yourself neutralized."

"I will not be an errand boy for him or anybody!" Eric shouted.

Dalton strode into the office and shut the door with a bang. "Lower your voice, son. Some influential businessmen who meet with Raymond regularly are in this building and roam these halls all the time. Now what is going on?"

Trumaine faced Dalton. "A small disagreement about strategy."

"Hardly," Eric retorted. "Acting without my approval and deciding to misrepresent my position makes this disagreement anything but small. Did you see this article, Dad?" He handed Dalton a copy of the newspaper.

Dalton didn't take it. "I'm sure Trumaine did what he felt was best for you and the party. Don't be so hot-headed, son. After all, you don't win a war without firing shots. If we're going to get anywhere with the party, we have to be bold."

Eric became still as a statue. "You knew about this," he said in a quiet voice. It was not a question.

"Trumaine," Dalton said with a nod toward the door. He waited until the door closed behind him. "Now look, Eric, Raymond wants results. He isn't going to settle for some soft-peddle kind of approach."

"This is too much." Eric turned his back on Dalton.

Dalton went on. "And I agree with him. All those social agencies have accomplished is to give folks an excuse to do nothing and be nothing."

"You, Trumaine, and Senator Raymond, huh? Everybody is in agreement on what I should do. How about asking me?" Eric spun to face him and threw the paper down on his desk.

"The story was all ready in the works. You knew that. We added what we thought was pertinent information gathered in the last few weeks. Listen, if you're worried about that social worker—"

Eric's eyes flared with indignation. "Shani is angry and justifiably so. It's obvious you didn't care about getting facts, only smearing the community centers."

"Nothing in that paper is a lie, young man. Look at it again," Dalton said, his voice sharp and defensive. "You've said as much about these social programs time and again."

Eric hung his head. "Why did you do this, Dad? To go behind my back and attack the woman I love..." He sank down into his chair.

Dalton gave a grunt of cynicism. "The woman you love. How many women have you been through since college? You averaged about two a year."

"Dad—"

"Tell me their names," Dalton pointed an index finger at him.

"Dad, you don't understand—"

"That's what I thought. Listen, here, boy. I worked long and hard to give my children what I never had. I won't see you throw away your career. Now if you take time to consider, you'll see I'm right." Dalton sat back in his chair. He wore a look of stern paternalism, the look of a father who was used to being obeyed and did not doubt he would be.

Eric sat up straight. He stared hard at his father for several seconds. "Don't ever talk down to me like that again. I'm way past being ten years old. No one, including you, will dictate to me how I conduct my career. Or my private life."

"You watch your mouth, son. And as for Ms. Moore, she's hardly more than a passing fancy." Dalton sat forward, his knuckles taut from gripping the arms of the chair. "She's not for you."

"Shani Moore is one of the finest women in the world. Don't ever disrespect her again," Eric continued ignoring his father's wrathful scowl. His voice was harsh. "I'm going to fire Trumaine and issue a statement denouncing this article."

"Now wait a minute young man!" Dalton jumped up. "I won't stand for any such thing!"

"You don't have a choice, Dad. I make my own decisions. You taught me that." Eric returned his father's look of fury with a steady gaze.

"But, your political career will be over in this state. You won't be able to get any legislation through. Don't be a fool, boy!" Dalton rubbed a large hand over his eyes. "This woman has got you behaving irrationally."

"That's enough!" Eric shouted causing his father's head to jerk up with shock. "My feelings for Shani have nothing to do with it. That article was underhanded. I want no part of such tactics. We have nothing else to talk about."

Dalton stood with his hands at his side balled into fists. He was the picture of impotent fury. "I thought you had more sense. Don't come crawling to me when you realize how stupid you've been." He stormed from the office.

Eric slumped back into his chair feeling exhausted. How could his father know so little about him? How could he not see how much Shani meant to him? Eric went over in his mind the talks he'd had with Dalton about her. All the time his father was pretending to understand. And now because of Dalton, he may have lost Shani. He pounded the desk top with his fist

"You all right, Senator Aucoin?" Nedra, his secretary, peered around the door frame. She appeared ready to take flight if need be.

Eric wiped a palm over his face and sighed. "Yeah sure, Nedra. Hold all my calls." He turned on the computer on his desk. "I've got a lot of work to do."

For the rest of the day, he lost himself in work. At least he could take control of one part of his life that had gone awry. Eric was determined to make a positive difference in the upcoming legislation, and do it the right way. Programs that were not helping the people they were designed for must be changed or eliminated so the money could reach the community. With shrinking resources and a backlash from the middle-class, excesses and abuses would have to end.

But Shani was never far from his mind no matter how hard he tried to banish her. He could smell the sweet scent of her skin or hear her laugh it seemed. More than once he stared at the monitor for long periods without seeing it. A cold empty feeling settled inside his chest. One he feared would be there for a long time. What a sorry end to the old year and a grim beginning to the new one. What would he have to celebrate December thirty-first at midnight?

Chapter 7

Outside the wind blew making the already forty-degree temperature feel more like below freezing. Shani and Terrilyn agreed they were tired of turkey and dressing. They sat in China Gardens waiting on their lunch orders.

"Brendon came with me to Angola. He and J.J. talked the whole time." Shani stirred the hot tea in her cup.

"That's great." Terrilyn stared at her.

"Yeah. Even with J.J. still behind bars, feels like those wounds in my family are really healing now. Brendon is genuinely proud of how J.J. has taken college courses."

"When will J.J. get out?" Terrilyn said.

"Hopefully before March. It looks good for him. At last he's got some reason for hope." Shani smiled for a moment before her lips sagged down again.

"He's a smart guy. Sounds like he got a made up mind to move in a better direction. I'm happy for him, Brendon, and for you."

Shani nodded. "At least Christmas was good for them this year. I mean for us." She avoided returning Terrilyn's gaze. "Don't start."

"What did I say?" Terrilyn held out both hands.

"It's what you're about to say. Don't go there, Terrilyn." Shani shot her a warning glance before staring back into her tea again.

"I just think you're being too hasty."

"Terrilyn, it's no use." Shani's eyes mirrored the hurt she felt. "Eric and I just can't make it. I was kidding myself that he really cared about me. You'd think Robert would have taught me a lesson."

"Hey, now. Don't be so down on yourself."

"Another New Year's Eve sitting at home eating popcorn and drinking sparkling fruit juice. Oh, well. At least I won't feel all tired out from partying and drinking all night," Shani said with a laugh devoid of humor.

"I'm putting my foot down this year, girlfriend. You are coming to the Circle of Friends Social Club's New Year's Eve party at the Hilton. I'm sure Jamal can hook you up with one of his buddies." Terrilyn's boyfriend of the moment was a fun-loving high school coach.

Shani's head whipped back and forth. "Forget it. I'm not interested in a blind date."

"Just one night of dancing and having a good time. That's all the commitment either of you need to make. What do say?"

"Well..." Shani mentally ran through a list of ways to be diplomatic yet firm. She didn't want to hurt Terrilyn's feelings. After all, she was only trying to help. No one else knew just how miserable New Year's Eve had been for her last year. But go on a date? No, she couldn't do it.

"Have mercy, look who just walked in and he's headed this way," Terrilyn said in a hurried whisper.

"Two lovely ladies. How are you, Shani?" Robert leaned down and kissed her forehead. "Hello, Terrilyn." He spoke with practiced charm.

Terrilyn stared at him with an impassive expression to show she was not moved. "Hi."

"Hello, Robert." Shani wished he would leave soon. "How are you?"

"Can't complain. This is still your favorite place to eat I see. I don't get over this way much since I moved to my new condo." Robert smiled at them. His manner suggested he was in a talkative mood.

"Really? Where?" Terrilyn said. She jumped when

Shani's foot kicked her ankle beneath the table.

Robert sat down next to Shani in the booth and got comfortable. "Those new luxury units on Concord Avenue. Three bedrooms, two and a half baths, and covered parking. You should see it." He stared at Shani for several seconds.

"So how is Claudia?" Shani shot back. "With her talents, she must have helped you decorate."

"I haven't seen Claudia in a while. Terrilyn, could you give us a minute?" Robert spoke with a delicate tone that implied she was a woman of understanding who would not refuse.

"I've got to visit the ladies' room anyway." Terrilyn screwed up her face when she turned away from him.

"What was that all about, Robert? We don't have a thing to talk about." Shani did not bother to look at him.

"Let's at least be on good terms if not friends. I'll settle for that if I have to." Robert put an arm around the back of the seat. "Not a day goes by that I don't regret behaving like such a fool. Let me make it up to you, baby."

Shani rubbed her temples. How easy it would be to give in. She was so tired of being angry. And he had helped her get through some rough days after the death of her mother. "Friends are all we can be now, Robert."

"I just don't want you to hate me. Let's call a truce, deal?" Robert leaned close to her.

Shani gazed at him for several seconds. "Deal." She blinked when he pressed his lips to hers.

"Still sweet," Robert grinned at her.

Shani pushed him away in time to see Eric standing at the cash register with a take-out bag. He was frozen in the act of handing money to the cashier.

To her horror, he headed straight for them.

"Hello, Shani. Guess I don't have to ask how you're doing," Eric said. His brown eyes sparkled with resentment. His gaze flickered to Robert. "Pretty well, I see."

Shani swallowed hard. "Hi." Then she got angry. Why should she feel guilty? Eric Aucoin did not own her. He could take his attitude and stuff it. "I'm doing quite well as a matter of fact." She lifted her chin in defiance.

"Robert Saucier, Senator. Nice to meet you." Robert was the picture of a smug, triumphant suitor as he stuck out his hand.

Eric stared at his hand for a second then glanced past Robert to Shani. "Right."

Robert dropped his hand. Still smiling, he broke the long moment of silence that stretched between them. "I've been following you're career with a lot of interest"

Eric shifted his focus back on Robert. He looked at him with open dislike. "Have you really?"

"Oh yes. It takes a lot of guts to be a black conservative, especially in this state. I mean, helping dismantle all those programs black leaders fought for long and hard, some even died. Yes, sir. Lots of nerve." Robert wore the ghost of a smile.

"Apparently Senator Aucoin thinks all those people were wrong and he's right. Everyone should pull themselves up by their bootstraps. The problem is, most poor people don't even have boots," Shani said.

"I think sometimes we don't give our people enough credit for being able to achieve before we jump in to help them. But I don't want to debate this here. Shani, I'll call you later. We need to talk," Eric said in a strained voice.

"Baby, don't forget we're going over to my place later for coffee and brandy," Robert put in before she could answer. He sat down, put a possessive arm around Shani and looked up at Eric. "I've just got a new condo and a new sound system. Shani is crazy about my collection of rhythm and blues classics."

Shani's anger at Eric won out over her urge to put Robert in his place. "Goodbye, Eric. I'm sure you have to rush off to continue the conservative revolution." Her voice was pure venom.

Eric stood clutching the bag of food so tight, his hands shook. He whirled around and walked away with long strides. Terrilyn, who had watched the scene from a distance, came back to the table.

"Whew! I thought we were going to have a big problem there for a while," Terrilyn mumbled. She watched Eric push the door so hard as he left it banged against the wall. "Mercy!"

"Well, ladies. Shall we order?" Robert was in high spirits. He rubbed his hands together.

Shani gave him a cutting look. "I've lost my appetite. Come on, Terrilyn." She tried to get past him.

"Hey, but I..." Terrilyn pointed to the hovering waitress ready to take their order. She stopped when Shani's eyes flashed her a warning. "Yeah, I'm not so hungry."

"Wait a minute, babe. Come on over to my place." Robert put his arm around Shani's waist and put his lips close to her ear. "You know it's true. You used to love sipping brandy and listening to Luther Vandross on my CD player."

Shani lifted her face to his. Her lips curved into an inviting smile. "Robert, there's only one thing wrong with that scene. *You*." She shoved him aside and headed out of the restaurant with Terrilyn right behind her.

"Oowee, girl," Terrilyn said in a voice breathless from giggling. "You're on a roll today."

"Yeah, and it's all downhill." Shani got in the passenger seat of Terrilyn's Honda Accord. "As if I wasn't feeling bad enough. Both of the men who've used me show up at once. A nice reminder of what an idiot I've been." Her bottom lip trembled.

"Stop that. They're the idiots, not you. Eric for letting his stupid politics get in the way of holding onto a fantastic woman, and Robert... Honey, we don't have time to list all the things wrong with that sorry excuse for a man." Terrilyn gave Shani a pat on the shoulder and started the car.

"But I chose them both, Terrilyn. What does that say about me?" Shani turned to her desperate for an answer.

Terrilyn turned to her. "It means you can make a mistake like anybody else. I've been there."

"But in this case, my heart was stomped on. Twice." Shani wiped her eyes with tissues from a dispenser in Terrilyn's car. "But I'm not going to walk around feeling sorry for myself. They can both get stuffed."

"Good for you, girl. And to start to top it off, let's have a blast at one of the finest parties in town. What about it?" Terrilyn winked at her.

Shani sniffed a couple of times. "Why not? Sure. Count me in."

"Fantastic! We're going bring the New Year in right, girlfriend."

Shani smiled at her. Terrilyn chattered about the parties being given and how they could attend more than one. Shani nodded in all the right places, but her mind was far away. The way Eric's eyes had clouded with contempt when he looked at her cut like a knife.

Any deep secret hopes that she and Eric could be together were now dashed. But she would go on without him. She had no choice.

***

"We've got a serious problem." Paulette closed the door to Shani's office. "My'iesha."

Shani felt a stab of fear. She knew what Paulette was going to say, but she asked anyway. "She saw the article?"

Paulette nodded yes. "She's convinced you know."

"I don't understand." Shani frowned at her.

"That she was in on the stealing around here. She was giving the merchandise to her last no-good man for a while. And he would fence it. She's ranting and raving that you stabbed her in the back."

Shani's eyes were wide with shock. "My'iesha is stealing from the center?"

"Not now, no. But in the first two months after she started the program. Then she left that low life and started to straighten out her life."

"Just when you think things can't get worse, they do." Shani closed her eyes and massaged her temples.

"Now she's all paranoid. She's still smoking weed, I'm afraid. I hope we can work through this—" Paulette spread her hands. She was cut short by My'iesha's entrance.

"You paid me back, huh? Told a damn reporter all that stuff." My'iesha stood with feet apart in an aggressive stance just inside the door.

"The article didn't say you gave them information for one thing." Shani spoke in a calm voice. "Most of it came from those conservative legislators. It said so in the article. Let's talk about this without shouting or accusations."

My'iesha strode farther into the room. "You been runnin' around with one of them legislators, too. Didn't think I knew. Yeah, I know that and a lot more. You been feedin' him all that crap."

"Why would I do something to hurt the center? You know how hard we've worked together for everything we have here. It doesn't make any sense." Shani could see by the wild look in her eyes that logic would not pierce the fog of suspicion.

"My'iesha, please. You need to go into detox like we talked about. There's a bed available." Paulette moved between them.

My'iesha grabbed Paulette by the arm and yanked her out of the way. She jabbed a finger at Shani. "LeVar been right about you all the time. Now he's gonna be after me thinkin' I ratted him out to the cops. I gotta find him so he'll know the truth."

Shani didn't go closer. My'iesha would feel cornered and might lash out with violence. "If LeVar does think that, then you should try to stay far away from him. He won't believe you, My'iesha. When the police don't come after him, maybe he'll know you didn't inform on him."

"I'm through listenin' to you. LeVar been the only one I could count on. He's gonna take good care of me." My'iesha walked backward looking from Shani to Paulette. "You two are always plottin' somethin'. Well, it won't work. You hear me? I'm not gonna be your chump no more!"

Shani took one cautious step toward her. "My'iesha, let us help you."

My'iesha spun around and stomped out. The sound of her pounding footsteps echoed down the hall. Paulette and Shani stood still for a full minute before they both slumped down into chairs with despondent sighs.

Paulette looked at Shani. "You think he'll hurt her?"

"You kidding? He's beaten her up for less than this."

"I knew the answer. Guess I was hoping you'd say something different."

"And I don't think she'll have to go looking for him. LeVar will find her. We've got to do something. But I don't know what." Shani raked fingers through her hair.

"Let's get some of the other staff in here. They've hit bottom before." Paulette referred to several counselors who were recovered addicts. "They might have some ideas." Paulette dialed the phone.

"Okay," Shani said. She stared down at the newspaper article. "Eric Aucoin should know just how dangerous playing politics at the expense of these people can be. He and his kind are despicable. If something happens to that young woman..."

Shani could only think of how self-involved she had been. Thinking only of herself and how much she missed him. The real consequences of his actions hit home now. She must see Eric as another foe. Paulette's voice, low and urgent, brought her back from her somber thoughts.

"They'll be down in about ten minutes," Paulette hung up the phone.

"Okay. But I intend for Senator Aucoin to take responsibility for his part in all this." Shani punched the buttons on the phone. "Yes, may I speak to Senator Aucoin. This is Shani Moore. Hello, Eric. I'm ready to talk."

***

Eric sat across from Detective McElroy Landry in the most popular coffee house in town. The Coffee Cafe was buzzing with activity as early morning customers came in for cafe au lait or strong dark roast south Louisiana coffee. Mac and he had been good friends since they played college football together. Now Mac was a respected narcotics cop.

"How's it going, Mac," Eric said.

"Doing what I can against the forces of evil. I haven't seen you since the last time you were on duty doing your reserved police officer thing. How's it going?" Mac straddled a chair making it look child-sized under his tall frame.

Eric grinned. "Pretty good. I managed a few rounds over the past months. But I'm going to have to give it up though. Too busy."

"The hazards of being an emerging statesman I guess," Mac teased.

When they both got coffee orders, Eric got down to business. "What do you know about a LeVar Stewart, Mac?" he said in a low voice leaning both elbows on the table.

Mac's thick black eyebrows went up a notch. His pleasant ebony face was transformed in an instant to a solemn mask.

"He went from a nobody to drug king pin just a few years short of his twentieth birthday. He did it by taking out anybody who stood in his way." Mac shrugged. "The man is a one-man crime wave."

"Damn," Eric said.

"You planning to make him and his kind a political issue?"

"It's personal." Eric shook his head when he saw Mac's eyes go opaque with worry. "Not me. Someone close to me is afraid he's going to hurt a young

119

woman."

"You got a name?"

"Yeah, My'iesha Campbell. She was in a drug treatment program until recently. You saw an article in the paper about the community centers?" Eric stared down into the creamy liquid in his mug.

"Uh-huh. You did some kinda investigation about theft and bad management. I skimmed over it before going to the sports section as usual." Mac grinned.

"Well, my former assistant gave a lot of the information for that article without my approval. He even went so far as to mention this young woman," Eric said.

"Not good."

"It gets worse. This Stewart guy now thinks she informed on him."

Mac let out a low whistle. "That is very bad news, my brother. LeVar is vicious when he even *thinks* someone's done him wrong."

"Look, Mac, I feel responsible for her being in danger. I should have kept Trumaine on a short leash," Eric said tapping the table top with a large fist. "But now that the damage is done, I've just got to do something about it. Can you help?"

Mac rubbed his chin. "Give me a minute." He got up and went outside to his car. Once inside, he started talking into his cell phone.

Eric glanced around the bright dining room. Early morning sunshine splashed through the wide windows giving everything and everyone a golden, happy glow. He thought of Shani's smile, a smile he had not seen for some time now. At least not for him. How his spirits had risen when she called only to plunge at her words of condemnation. Eric still felt the sting of hearing her controlled voice stabbing through the phone. In that moment, all his explanations about the report and his party actions shriveled up into nothingness. A young woman's life was in jeopardy because he had been careless. Staring out to the parking lot, he prayed Mac would find a way to save My'iesha. The tall man turned a few female heads when he came back into the restaurant.

Mac placed the cell phone next to his now cold mug of coffee. "I've got good news and bad news. The good news is LeVar is wanted on a warrant, and we're already looking to take him down. This time he could get a hefty sentence if he's convicted. That's a big if, but better than nothing."

Eric checked his rising hope. "What's the bad news?"

"There was a drive-by shooting. Three guys shot, two dead and the third one is in critical condition. Word is, LeVar and his gang are responsible. He's on a revenge rampage."

Eric hung his head. Like Shani, he wanted a way to stop the killing. Somehow leaders along the political spectrum must agree to approaches they could all support.

"And one of his former girls is supposed to be a target."

"My'iesha?" Eric's head jerked up. He felt anxiety tighten in his chest at Mac's sober nod. "What can we do? There's got to be a way to help her."

"Maybe she ought to leave town for a while. That way we won't have to worry about her getting killed before he's caught."

"Shani doesn't know where she is. In fact, My'iesha is looking for LeVar. She thinks she can explain herself to him," Eric said.

"Definitely a bad idea. That's like helping a rattlesnake sink his fangs into a major artery." Mac sat in thought for several minutes. "I've got an idea, but it involves your friend. Does she have any clue where My'iesha could be?"

"Maybe. But I don't want Shani put in any danger, Mac." Eric felt even greater fear at the possibility that she could be hurt as well.

"What's your idea, Detective? I'm Shani Moore. Sorry I'm late." Shani ignored the stunned look on Eric's face.

"What are you doing here?" Eric pulled out a chair for her next to him. A faint whiff of her fragrance stirred sweet memories.

"You told me about meeting here with Detective Landry, remember?" Shani turned to Mac. "Now, about that idea?"

Eric's cell phone beeped. "It's my office."

While Eric walked off to call in, Mac explained his plan to Shani. She listened and interrupted only to ask a couple of questions. Mac paused mid-sentence to stare at Eric with a frown.

"Something is very wrong. Eric looks like he just got hit by a truck," Mac said.

Eric came back, his face stiff with grief. "My mother has been taken very ill. Dad's at the emergency room with her. I've got to go."

Shani put a hand on his arm. "I'm so sorry, Eric. Can I do anything?"

Eric's hand closed on hers. "I'll call you later?" His eyes searched hers for comfort.

"Of course," Shani replied.

"Let me know how your mama is doing, man. You know how I feel about that special lady." Mac put a hand on Eric's shoulder.

Eric could only nod in gratitude before hurrying off. Shani and Mac watched him leave. Both wore frowns of concern for him and his parents.

"Like my grandma says, if it ain't one thing, it's two," Mac said.

Shani sighed. "And that's the truth."

***

"She's going to be all right, son." Dalton gripped Eric's arms tight. "It was a very mild stroke." His face showed the strain of fear at losing the woman he loved.

"But she couldn't talk or move her right arm," Eric said. His insides churned at the thought of his mother suffering.

"Her speech came back though it's still a little slurred. And she can move her arm, just not too much." Dalton let go of Eric and twisted his hands together as he talked. "She's going to bounce back. Of course she's going to need physical and speech therapy. She'll be back to her old self in no time."

Eric could see that his father was trying to reassure himself. Dalton's hand shook as he wiped his brow with a monogrammed linen handkerchief. For the first Ume, Eric realized how much his parents were a part of each other. All day, Eric had waited with his father for the test results. Now in the twilight of early evening, the white lights of the small waiting seemed eerie and forbidding. He put his hand on Dalton's back to console him.

"Of course she will. Mama is a fighter." Eric hoped his face did not show the uncertainty he felt. "Let's go in."

The hospital room door swished open and Dalton went inside ahead of Eric. At first it seemed Adeline was asleep in the darkened room. The only light came from the television.

Dalton scowled. "Now who left that on," he said in a harsh whisper. He reached for the remote that hung over the bed rail.

"Me. Don't to-ouch it," Adeline said. "It's Wednesday and I never miss m-my favorite shows." Her lips curved into a mischievous smile. There was a slight droop to one side of her mouth. "Come on in here you two, and give me some sugar."

Dalton leaned down brushing a tendril of hair from her face as he did so. He pressed his lips to hers for a long moment, his eyes closed. Eric almost felt a need to leave them alone. The tenderness and love between them was a palpable thing filling the air, making the antiseptic hospital atmosphere seem less impersonal. Seeing the bond between his parents, Eric felt a pang deep inside. How he needed to make things right with Shani. There was no doubt in his mind that she was the one he wanted, needed, to share his life and his heart.

"How's my sweet thing feeling?" Dalton continued brush her hair with his fingers.

"Like a weak kitten. I hope you didn't forget to bring my blue nightgown. Soon as they take out this IV, I'm going to wear my own things. There's my baby." Adeline held up her left arm to welcome Eric.

"Hey, darlin'. You look marvelous." Eric smiled and kissed her cheek.

"Don't lie to me, Eric Paul Aucoin. I look like hell." Adeline shook a finger at his nose. She gazed at him, then Dalton. "But so do you. Both of you got those smiles plastered in place trying not to look scared."

"We were, but now we've gotten the good news that—"

"That I ha-ad a str-roke? What do you call *good* news?" Adeline said with a grunt.

Eric cleared his throat and forced cheer into his

voice. "Well, not that of course. But it wasn't as serious as it could have been. The doctor says—"

"That they can remove the blockage and reduce the chance of another one. I know. They've been poking and pulling on me since I got here. They took so much blood, I was beginning to wonder if Dracula wasn't on staff here." Adeline shifted on the raised bed.

Eric gave a low laugh. He was encouraged to hear his mother joking. "Those lab techs do only seem to come at night or early in the morning before the sun comes up. Seriously, Mama, Doctor Mills is very optimistic you can make a full recovery."

"Yeah, sweetie. We'll be doing the swing out by the spring fraternity dance. You wait and see." Dalton held his wife's hand.

"Now there's a reason to have some therapist ordering me around. Going to that dance so I can watch Odessa Trahan paw you at every opportunity." Adeline pursed her lips. "She's tried to get her hands on him since we were in college. But I snapped him up."

Dalton gave a groan. "You gonna start on that. It's been over thirty years, Adeline." His eyes were alight with amusement to share this old argument they'd had for years, never in anger but to tease each other.

"Well, she can just retract those claws because I'm not going anywhere for a long time." She caressed her husband's jaw. "So get that worried look off your face." Her voice was soft.

Dalton held her hand to his cheek. His eyes filled with unshed tears. "We'll be fine, you and me."

"Yes, dear. Just fine." Adeline's eyebrows came together, giving her a severe look. "Now there is some unfinished business between you two."

"Adeline, don't you let that weigh on your mind.

You've got to concentrate on getting well." Dalton blinked. A look of guilt crossed his rugged features.

Eric took his father's cue. "Yeah, Mama. The most important thing is your health."

"Hu-ush up. Dalton," she said, fixing him with a look of censure. "You owe your son an apology."

"Now, Adeline, don't get worked up." Dalton patted her hand.

"Dalton Augustin Aucoin, tell him," Adeline said in a voice of quiet strength.

Dalton took a deep breath. "Forgive me, son. I had no right to interfere the way I did." He stared down at the floor.

"And?" Adeline urged him on with a sharp nod.

"And ... I was wrong to go behind your back and help Trumaine feed all that stuff to the news reporter." Dalton scratched his head with a nervous movement of his hand.

Adeline sighed and settled back with a pleased expression. "That's a start. Eric, tell your father he's forgiven. Go on."

"Mama, we—"

Adeline made an attempt to sit up by holding on to rail. "Don't ma-ake me-e get up out of this bed, boy."

Eric's eyes widened with alarm. He stepped forward and placed his hands on both her shoulders. Dalton gave her a gentle but firm push back against the pillows.

"Adeline, you are the most willful little woman." Dalton gazed up at Eric. His eyes were full of emotion. "Best do as you're told, son. Am I forgiven?"

"Sure," Eric said in a voice strangled with unspoken feelings for the man he admired more than anyone else. "Sure you are, Dad." He hugged Dalton's neck.

Adeline nodded at them. "Now talk to each other." Her eyes were already half-closed. "I'm going to take a nap. I can rest easier now."

Eric and Dalton left only after her low, regular breathing assured them she was asleep. They returned to the small waiting room down the hall.

"My apology wasn't just to keep your mama from getting upset. I had no right to come between you and Shani. It was wrong." Dalton looked away. "Adeline means the world to me. When you find the woman who makes you feel like a king even when the whole world is beating you down, well there's just no way to replace that."

"I believe you, Dad." Eric was moved.

"Is there anything I can do to make things right between you two?"

"Thanks, but no. Something was bound to test our relationship." Eric lifted his shoulders. "Maybe it's just as well we broke up. Could be our differences are just too big."

"You think so?" Dalton rubbed his chin and gazed off into the distance. "Maybe, maybe not."

Eric's head lowered, his chin touching the top of his open collar. "I'm afraid it's not, Dad. Anyway," he said looking up again, "at least there's good news about Mama. Listen, why don't you go home and rest? I'll stay here tonight."

"Humm? Oh no, I don't . . . Well okay. I'll go take a shower and change. But I'll be back in a few hours." Dalton slapped Eric's back. "You take the early shift. I'll be back by ten or ten-thirty."

"But you've been up since four this morning," Eric protested. "The last thing I need is for both of you to be sick."

"Trust me, son. My place is with Adeline. Now go on in there. That lounge chair is surprisingly comfortable. My thoughtful secretary is on her way with some food for me. You eat it. I'll get something on the way home." Dalton pulled him along.

"I'm not all that hungry."

"You will be. Now quit arguing with me. When I'm through, things are going to work out right." Dalton gave a cheerful wave goodbye before stepping through the open doors of the elevator. "You'll see."

"What?" Eric blinked in puzzlement at his words. "Dad, wait a minute."

The doors clicked shut leaving him to wonder about the mysterious grin his father wore.

***

"Sure you want to go through with this?" Mac said to Shani. He glanced around with an uneasy grimace on his dark features. "This isn't the safest place to be in the daytime, much less after dark."

They sat in his unmarked car outside a rundown boarding house on East Boulevard. Several blocks down the street a group of young men stood on a corner laughing and shoving each other. Cars drove up to them then sped off after a hasty transaction. Rap music blared from a ramshackle house about a block down East Boulevard behind them. Mac took his eyes off the boarding house only to check their surroundings through the rearview mirrors.

"We both know that My'iesha could disappear fast. If she's here, I want to be with you to talk to her." Shani was so intent on what she would say to My'iesha, she did not feel afraid for herself. Her fear was for the young woman who teetered on the edge of being another murder statistic.

"Let's just hope LeVar isn't up there with her.

Things could get ugly real quick." Mac slipped a hand inside the wool blazer to pat his shoulder holster. He shot a look of fury at the group of young men. The fifth car to stop in the last fifteen minutes pulled away. "Wish I could bust those little punks."

"When I see guys like that, it makes me wish I knew the answer to harness all that potential. All going to waste on a street corner or in a prison cell." Shani felt a pall wash over her. The dreary houses with litter strewn in the front yards and in the gutters made for a dark scene. She did not wonder children growing up here would do desperate, dangerous things to escape.

Mac grunted. "More often these days, they end up in a body bag." He pointed to a window. "Look, a light just went on. Somebody's home. You ready?"

Shani's heart thumped, but she put her hand on the door handle. "Yes." She unwrapped the woolen scarf around her neck and let it slide down to the seat.

Mac put his arm out. "Eric is going to kill me when he finds out I brought you here. Maybe we should put this off."

"We've been over that, Mac. He's got enough on his mind with Mrs. Aucoin being ill."

Mac sucked air into his lungs. "Yeah, he's been at the hospital with only a couple of breaks for the last twenty- four hours. Thankfully Ms. Adeline is doing so good."

Shani thought of the anguish in Eric's hazel eyes after hearing the news that his mother was hospitalized. His pain had been her pain. And she shared his joy and relief when he called to tell her Mrs. Aucoin's condition was improving. But the joy was tempered by the knowledge that they would not, could not be together. The newspaper story and the effects of it stood between them like a stone wall. Shani again thought of how foolish she'd been to think their differences could be overcome. Maybe love was not enough. Once they left the sweet haze of their romantic cocoon, the real world slammed them back into being on opposing sides with a vengeance. And they had to live in the real world. The real world of Shani's commitment to programs Eric wanted to destroy. She felt the familiar sadness at the thought. Now she must move ahead and stop feeling sorry for herself. Shani stared at the weathered wooden porch that sagged on one side.

"So we agreed not to call Eric. Besides, we're just going in to talk My'iesha out of this mess."

"It's up to you." Mac continued to watch the window.

"I just hope I can. LeVar knows how to sweet talk needy young women starved for affection. If he's gotten to her..."

"From all you've said, he got to her a while ago. Now the question is, can she break free?" Mac followed her gaze. "And will she listen to you?"

Shani opened the car door. "We're about to find out."

At that moment, a shout went up from the group of young men.

"Who done stole my money!" a loud voice boomed.

Curses rang out. Mac muttered a few choice words and kicked open the driver's side door of the sedan. Shani craned her neck around to see two men pounding each other and two others jump into the fray. Mac barked the location of the disturbance into his police radio unit

"Looks like crowd control is going to be needed for this. Better get over there before some fool starts shooting. Stay here. I'll let the uniforms take over and be back."

More people had gravitated to the scene. He covered the three blocks with long strides. A marked police car came from the opposite direction lights flashing.

Shani sat for fifteen minutes before she began to worry that My'iesha would run if she noticed all the activity; especially if she saw the police car. After several more minutes of silent debate and courage gathering, Shani decided to enter the boarding house.

"After all, how bad can it be? There's a light in the entrance," she murmured.

Her footsteps across the porch sounded too loud. She pushed open the door and entered a hallway lit with a naked bulb set in the ceiling. The worn stairway railing wobbled as she climbed the steps.

***

Eric sat next to the hospital bed. He stared into the darkness outside. His mood matched the grim looking shadows thrown by the building onto the ground below. The happiness he felt was not complete. With a glance at his sleeping mother, he felt a jab of guilt to be thinking of himself at such a time. Yet he couldn't help it. Shani had been glad to hear from him, of that he was certain. But the reserve in her voice over the telephone hurt more than a little. For a brief moment, he wanted to believe they could find a way back to each other. When she looked at him that day he got the call about his mother, her eyes were filled with emotion. He felt the familiar pull between them. Now he realized the loss of something precious. And it seemed Shani would not be able to forgive him.

"Well hello there. Don't tell me you haven't been home or gotten something to eat." Adeline's voice was alert though she'd been sleeping on and off for most of the time since being admitted to the hospital.

"Hello, beautiful." Eric got up and kissed her forehead. "How're you feeling? Can I get you anything?"

"Some water, please." Adeline sipped through the straw. "Umm, that's better. Other than feeling a little weak, I'm just fine." She put the plastic cup aside and stared at her son. "Goodness, you look beat."

Eric straightened his shirt collar and sweater. "I'm okay."

"Where's Dalton?"

"He's down the hall on the phone. Business calls. He didn't want to disturb you."

"I see. I look a sight." Adeline began to brush her hair while looking into a small mirror set in the combination table and vanity positioned next to the bed. "What's your excuse?"

"I don't understand." Eric sat back down.

"Eric, you can't deceive me. For the first time, I saw your eyes gleam in a very special way just at the mention of a woman's name. Now that gleam is gone."

"Mama, worry about my problems. You've got to think of getting better. I'll survive."

"Humph, I wonder."

Eric tried to make his voice sound light, but knew he'd failed. "You've got therapy sessions and a new diet to follow. And I expect you to obey the doctor's orders."

"Don't lecture me, young man. I know exactly what I have to do, thank you very much. And don't try to change the subject." Adeline shook a finger at him.

"Have you spoken to Shani?"

"Yes, she sends best wishes and told me to tell you she's glad to hear you're doing so well." Eric turned his face away.

"How sweet. But that's not what I'm talking about, and you know it. What about you two? Have you made up?"

"Mama ..." Eric drew in a sharp breath. "We're not going to make up. It's over. The most we can be are cordial acquaintances."

"What nonsense."

"Mama, you don't understand."

Adeline put the hair brush down. "Ha! I was learning about love before you were even thought of, sugar. And don't tell me you can't make it because she's a liberal social worker and you're a conservative. All silliness."

"It's not so simple as labels. It's how we act on our convictions."

"Eric Paul Aucoin, you must be trying real hard to be stupid because there are no dumb people in our family. You sure didn't inherit it from my side." Adeline squinted at him.

"Mama!—"

"I don't want to hear it," she broke in. "Sitting around here with that 'poor pitiful me' look on your face. Both of you share a drive to do the best thing for people, that's why she's a social worker and why you went into politics. Maybe you disagree on the methods, but so what? You share the same values and have some of the same ideas."

"Hey, babe. What's up?" Dalton strolled in wearing a big smile when he saw Adeline awake and looking refreshed. He brushed his lips across hers.

Adeline's eyes twinkled at the sight of her husband. "Sit down. Maybe you can help talk sense to this child."

"Mama, Shani and I have some very real problems we can't overcome. I wish we could but, that's just the way it is." Eric felt an ache at his words. What he wanted to believe and reality were two different things. There was no denying that Shani could never feel the same for him.

"I don't think it has to be that way, son. She misses you just as much." Dalton spoke up.

"No, she doesn't." Eric shook his head. He was still turned away from them.

"Oh yes she does," Dalton said with a certain ring to his voice.

Eric faced him. "Why do you say that? Dad, you haven't been talking to her have you?" He wore a tense expression that threatened to turn into anger.

Dalton blinked. "Uh, I'm just saying... I bet she's missing you real bad. From the way you two were all lovey- dovey, I could tell she's as crazy about you as you are about her." He cleared his throat. "That's all I meant."

"Why don't we call her right now? I'd love to say hello." Adeline gestured toward the phone at her nightstand. She yawned. "These darn pills keep me sleepy. Hurry up before I doze off again."

Eric swallowed hard. He stood with his hand on the receiver for several seconds before picking it up. After the tenth ring, he hung up. "She's not there." A picture on the television caught his eye. "Turn up the sound, Dad."

A mug shot appeared on the screen as a reporter spoke. "Police believe this man, LeVar Stewart is responsible for the last drive by shooting in Easy Town. Crime Stoppers is offering a cash reward for information that leads to his arrest and conviction."

Eric remembered what Mac had said right before

he got the call at the restaurant about his mother. Shani had not been home twice before when he'd tried to call. He punched in the number to Mac's desk phone at the station.

"Hey, Eric." His partner, Bill, answered. "No, he went out after some woman tied up with this Stewart scum ball. Some ratty place on East Boulevard. How's Mrs. A?"

Eric answered him in a mechanical fashion before hanging up. His mind raced with terrible possibilities. He knew how much Shani wanted to save My'iesha. Could she be in danger now? And was she with Mac? East Boulevard was a high crime area well known to him. He had visited an angry group of people who lived there about efforts to clean it up.

"Eric, is anything wrong?" Adeline frowned up at him.

"No, Mama. Look, I'm going to find Shani." Eric gave her hand a quick squeeze.

"Oh, that's wonderful, dear. Don't let a good thing get away." Adeline waved at him, all ready she was struggling to keep her eyes open.

Dalton followed him to the door. "Something's wrong," he whispered. "Tell me what's going on."

Eric smiled. "Nothing, Dad. Really. Now take it easy. I'll be back in the morning, okay?" He patted his father's back and walked off before Dalton could say more.

***

"Honey, open the door please," Shani said in a low, urgent voice. "I know you're in there. My'iesha?"

"What you doin' here? Go way," My'iesha called back. She sounded tense.

Shani heard a thump and a furtive rustling sound.

135

"Let's talk. Just let me in for ten minutes."

"I'll see you at the center. Tomorrow maybe. Now go away." My'iesha seemed closer to the door.

"It's got to be now. I promise not to lecture you or stay for longer than ten minutes."

After a few seconds, there was the rattle of locks being opened. Slowly the door swung back into the room. My'iesha, looking drawn with dark circles under her eyes, peered out at her. Shani smiled and stepped inside. The door shut with a bang.

"What you want? Got no right harassing me like this," My'iesha rasped. Her whole body shook.

Shani approached but stopped short when My'iesha backed up against the wall. "I'm worried about you. LeVar is on a rampage. Word is out he intends to hurt you bad."

"He gonna listen to me," My'iesha said. "I'm gonna explain to him. I didn't tell the police nothin'. I swear." She rubbed her nose and sniffed hard several times.

"How many times have you used in the last day or so?" Shani moved closer, more concerned about getting her some help than being attacked. Still, she kept her arms by her sides in case My'iesha lashed out in a drug-induced rage.

"Get offa me," My'iesha warned as she inched away. "I mean it."

"Let me help you. LeVar shot two people that I know of in the last few days. Instead of trying to find him, you should be hauling butt hoping he doesn't find you." Shani planted her feet apart.

"I ain't listenin' to that crap. It's a bunch of lies just like in the newspaper. You and Senator Aucoin set me up!"

Shani shook her head. "You should know me better than that."

My'iesha's mouth turned down in a little girl expression of misery. Large tears rolled down her cheeks. "I thought you was my friend. Different from all them other social workers, psychologists, and stuff."

"I do want to help you. Just come with me." Shani stepped ever closer. She reached out her across the few inches between them.

My'iesha stared down at Shani's hand. In an instant, her face twisted with rage. "No! You ain't turnin' me in to go to jail. I ain't goin'."

She swung wild. The flat of her hand slapped Shani's shoulder with enough force to make her rock back. Shani shuffled back to regain her footing, but My'iesha lunged at her again.

"Stop it! My'iesha, stop!" Shani wrapped her arms around the thin frame. My'iesha tried to break loose from the tight lock, but Shani held her fast.

"Let go of me. Take your filthy, no-good hands off me," My'iesha sobbed. She struggled for a few minutes, but fatigue and emotion left her physically drained. "No, no, no," she cried in a sad sing-song voice as Shani cradled her.

Shani eased them both down onto the sagging bed. "It's going to be all right, sweetie. Shush now."

***

Eric parked on the opposite side of the street behind a dark green sedan. Everything looked quiet, too quiet. He glanced around looking for a sign of his friend or Shani then walked to Mac's car. His heart gave a lurch when he recognized Shani's woolen scarf on the floor in front of the passenger seat. With care, he climbed the steps to the boarding house. Stale cooking smells hit him when he opened the door leading to a dank hallway. Music and shouting came from behind several of the battered doors. Someone sang a popular rap song in a drunken fashion. One dim yellow bulb hung from a long wire to light it. A stairway of dark, scarred wood led up and to the right.

I hope Mac is up here with her. Eric climbed the steps wincing at the creaks that sounded loud enough to be heard miles away. A door cracked open to reveal the head of a middle-aged man. The man blinked at Eric with bloodshot eyes then shut the door real quick. Eric tried not to think about how many ways he could be ambushed as he continued up to the third floor. Mac's partner, distracted by another case, had told him where they expected to find My'iesha. When he got to the third-floor landing, he squinted in the darkness. He went to the fourth door with a rusty "3D" hanging at a lopsided angle. Muffled sobbing sent a chill through him.

"Shani?" He knocked hard. "Shani, are you there?" A bump and unrecognizable sounds from within pushed him into to panic. "Open up!" He slammed his shoulder against the peeling painted wood panel.

Shani jerked the door open. "Bring out every gangster within a five-mile radius, why don't you."

Eric stumbled into the room from the momentum of another attempt to batter his way in. "You all right? I heard crying like someone was hurt." He steadied himself and whirled around in a circle looking for danger.

"I'm fine," Shani said. She felt a rush of warmth at the sight of him on guard and ready to defend her. "It's just My'iesha and me."

"Oh." Eric looked a little embarrassed. But soon his eyes blazed with annoyance. "You shouldn't have come in here without Mac. LeVar could have been in here wired up and packing a gun. He wouldn't hesitate to shoot."

"You're right," Shani murmured.

"Taking crazy chances with your life like this is ..." Eric huffed in growing anger.

"Stupid, I know." Shani shut the door behind him. "I didn't stop to think. I was just so afraid that My'iesha would slip away from us. I didn't want to lose a chance to keep her from LeVar."

"Well, uh, yeah. No harm done since you're both safe." Eric lost steam, thrown off balance by her ready agreement with him. He gazed at My'iesha who sat staring at him with big dark eyes.

"Right," Shani said. She was amused by the confusion her meek response caused. "My'iesha, this is Senator Aucoin."

"Hi," My'iesha said in a soft whisper. She hugged herself and rocked.

Shani sat next to her again. She put her arm around My'iesha's thin shoulders. "He wants to help you, too."

"Then why did he tell lies to that reporter? He tryin' to get rid of the work program. And he got LeVar thinkin' I ratted him out to the cops." My'iesha shot an accusatory glance at Eric.

Eric sat down in one of two chairs part of an old dinette set "My'iesha, I'm sorry for the way that newspaper article was written. I didn't know about it, believe me." His jaw tightened at the reference to Trumaine.

"But you tryin' to close Mid-City down. I heard you say so on television." My'iesha's expression of distrust remained.

"No, not really. I just want to make sure the money gets to those it's intended to help." Eric gazed at Shani. "Mid- City is doing a fantastic job in Easy

Town. The records confirm that."

"Then they won't close down the jobs program or the drug counseling?" My'iesha leaned forward, wanting to believe but still wary. Her face showed the ravages of a lifetime of hopes dashed. She twisted a pulled thread of the oversized sweater that hung on her slight frame. "When I worked in that office, it was the first time I really started to think I could be somebody."

"No money has been cut off. And even though some may try to, I'll work damn hard to save it. It's one of the programs that's effective and saves money. Every person who makes it, pays taxes. That's what I'm going to say to the legislators." Eric looked at her. His strong jaw set with determination and genuine concern shown in his eyes. "We're all going to work hard to make sure the center keeps helping people. Okay?"

My'iesha looked to Shani for confirmation. At her nod she turned back to Eric. "Okay," My'iesha said in a more confident voice.

"Good, now let's get out of this place." Eric stood up.

Shani rose with her arm still around My'iesha. "I second that motion."

A knock shook the old door on its hinges. "Hey, girl. Open up. It's me, LeVar."

All three froze for several seconds. My'iesha gasped and shrunk back away from the door. Eric put a forefinger to his lips.

"I sent word by one of his boys for him to come here," My'iesha whispered low. Her voice seemed ring out.

"You in there, Leo told me." LeVar pulled at the door knob. "One way or the other, I'm comin' in," he barked. After several seconds, he changed his tone.

"Come on, baby. I got somethin' special just for my special lady. Don't I always treat you good? LeVar gives good love, don't he, baby?"

Eric walked to the window on tip toes. There was no escape that way. Maybe LeVar would be convinced the room was empty and leave. Eric glanced at Shani.

"Now what?" she lip synched to him.

Eric started toward them to respond when the door bounced inward with a boom. My'iesha shrieked and went limp with fright.

"I'm tired of messin' 'round. You hear me? Ain't nobody gonna screw up my business." LeVar kicked the door to punctuate each sentence.

Eric pushed the two women into a far corner. He crouched to the right of the door, fists raised. The flimsy lock popped loose as wood splintered around it. LeVar rushed into the room with one arm extended. Eric punched the side of his head causing it to snap back. LeVar staggered forward. Before he could recover, Eric swung both fist down on the back of his neck. The gun in LeVar's hand fell and slid across the floor. Shani crawled toward it. LeVar let out a groan of rage. He shook Eric from his back and started for her. Eric delivered a series of rapid punches that made LeVar's head bounce as though on springs. Eric rammed him into a wall with such force that the window panes rattled. LeVar slumped to the floor with a moan, his hand flailing the air in a vain attempt at defense. Suddenly Mac's tall frame was a silhouette in the doorway. He took in the scene with a quick professional gaze before his stance relaxed. He crossed to Eric.

"I'll take over from here, brother," Mac said.

Eric stepped back. "He's all yours," he said in a breathless voice.

Mac stood over LeVar, his gun in hand. "I got

141

more bad news for you, man. You're under arrest."

He motioned two uniformed police officers into the room. They handcuffed LeVar and rattled off his rights in a practiced monotone.

Eric went to Shani and My'iesha. "You both okay?" He scanned them both for evidence of injury.

"We're not hurt." Shani could feel My'iesha trembling. "I think we better get her to a hospital. She might be going into shock."

Mac led a paramedic inside the already crowded cramped room. "Here we go, ma'am. Let's get you checked out." He spoke in a soothing tone, very unlike the hard as steel cop he'd been only a few minutes earlier.

"You comin'?" My'iesha did not let go of Shani's arm.

"Sure, honey. You go on. I'll be there in a minute." Shani brushed back her hair. She turned to Eric and Mac. "Well, thank goodness for Buffalo Soldiers to the rescue."

"Aw, shucks ma'am," Mac said in an exaggerated Texas drawl. He grinned at her. "Don't mention it. Are you two okay? Wanna see the paramedics?"

"No," they said in unison.

"Well then, both of you get some rest. See you later."

He slapped Eric on the back before going off to confer with his lieutenant.

She hesitated before joining My'iesha in the Emergency Medical Services van. Shani gazed up at Eric.

"I'm going with her. She's scared—."

"Of course. I'll follow." Eric nodded. He did not reach with his hands, but looked at her with tenderness, reaching out with his heart.

"Will you?" Shani wanted to take a step toward

him but the memory of angry words, her angry words, held her in place. Had she any right to believe what she saw in his eyes?

"Anywhere, anytime." Eric wrapped her in his arms. "Just try and stop me," he murmured in her ear.

***

Attached to every chair placed around the tables scattered in the huge ballroom, colorful helium filled balloons danced and bounced as people passed. Elegantly dressed couples dipped and swayed to the soulful rhythm of a popular local band. Shani laughed out loud, less at the antics of a nearby couple who shimmied down to the floor in imitation of a long ago dance from their youth, than with the sheer joy of being happier than she could ever remember in her life. Feeling Eric's arms cradling her, she thought of how different this holiday was from a year ago. New Year's Eve 2011 was as sparkling as any champagne. And 2012 would burst forth bright with the promise of a new beginning. Looking up into his eyes, Shani felt lighter than the balloons.

"Having a good time?" Eric spoke close to her ear.

"I'm having a marvelous time, the time of my life." She pressed closer to him.

"Did I mention how beautiful you look in this sexy number?" Eric held her at arm's length. His gaze lingered on the low neckline of her emerald green satin bodice. The full black velvet skirt swished around her ankles.

"You're not half bad yourself." She gave him a wink. His broad shoulders and chest wore the tuxedo jacket with as much ease as any causal shirt.

"Thanks, my lady." He pulled her back close to him. "It's almost midnight. The new year is going to be wonderful."

"To think, only a few weeks ago things looked very bleak. But My'iesha is back on the right track and in treatment"

"That's great, babe. Having LeVar in jail and probably going to prison doesn't hurt," Eric said.

"Amen. Things are looking up for my family, too. My brothers are closer than ever. J.J. has a job waiting for him thanks to Brendon."

"And to think, my father actually tracked you down to say he was responsible for that article. So I have him to thank for this night. Yeah, family matters are looking good," Eric said, his voice filled with contentment

"The new year can't come fast enough for me." Shani snuggled closer to him.

"Me too," he murmured. "Yes, it looks like 2012 is going to be full of action for both of us."

' 'Yes, with the session coming up for you and me working on new programs with a scaled down budget"

"Oh, yeah. I guess that too," Eric said with a shrug.

Shani look up at him. "We're not talking about the same thing. What's up?"

"You'll find out," he said with the impish grin of a man with a secret

"Hey, everybody. Here's the count down." One of the party hosts called to the crowd from the microphone on the bandstand. A big screen television mounted high over their heads came on as the lights were dimmed. The ball, lit with red lights to look like a gigantic apple, in New York's Time Square started its descent.

"Seven, six, five," Shani and Eric yelled with the others. She molded her back to his chest feeling his rising excitement His hands crossed at her waist.

"One. Happy New Year!" Hundreds of voices blended with the sound of corks being popped and horns blowing.

"Happy New Year, baby," Eric whispered. His kiss was long and deep. "Will you marry me?"

Shani, all ready left breathless with the heat of desire, uttered a tiny cry. "Yes, yes." She placed both hands on his face and kissed him hard. "Yes!"

"Now, you're going to be very busy picking out your engagement ring and planning our wedding." He chuckled.

"That's the way to start a New Year." She laughed with him.

The band started another tune, and they swung in a circle. The sultry contralto of a female singer came through the speakers. As she sang, Shani felt as though the singer had chosen her song just for them. Shani, her cheek resting against Eric's solid shoulder, hummed along with the words "Caught Up in the Rapture of Love."

～ About the Author ～

Mix knowledge of voodoo, Louisiana politics and forensic social work with the dedication to write fiction while working each day as a clinical social worker, and you get a snapshot of author Lynn Emery. Lynn has been a contributing consultant to the magazine *Today's Black Woman* for three articles about contemporary relationships between black men and women. For more information visit:

Visit me on the web at:

www.lynnemery.com

Connect with me on:
Twitter: www.twitter.com/LEmeryWriter
Facebook: www.facebook.com/lynn.emery.author